The Short Stories Of Wilkie Collins

The short story is often viewed as an inferior relation to the Novel. But it is an art in itself. To take a story and distil its essence into fewer pages while keeping character and plot rounded and driven is not an easy task. Many try and many fail.

In this series we look at short stories from many of our most accomplished writers. Miniature masterpieces with a lot to say. In this volume we examine some of the short stories of Wilkie Collins.

William Wilkie Collins was born on January 8th 1824.

Bullied as a child his escape was to tell the bully a story each night before going to sleep. It proved to be quite an education.

Lauded as the Father of the Detective novel, Collins was the author of The Moonstone and The Woman In White among the thirty novels he wrote.

A great friend and colleague of Charles Dickens (who regularly published him in his own magazines) Collins was also a playwright and prolific author of short stories.

A sufferer of gout he used and became addicted to opium to combat the pain.

Writing at the time of the Franco-Prussian War in 1870 he stated, "I begin to believe in only one civilising influence – the discovery one of these days of a destructive agent so terrible that War shall mean annihilation and men's fears will force them to keep the peace."

Collins died on September 23, 1889 at 82 Wimpole Street, following a paralytic stroke. He is buried in Kensal Green Cemetery in London.

Collected here for your reading pleasure are a selection of chilling, disturbing, but always entertaining stories from a man at the top of his craft and always aware of his effect on the minds of us mere mortals.

Many of these stories are also available as an audiobook from our sister company Word Of Mouth. Many samples are at our youtube channel http://www.youtube.com/user/PortablePoetry?feature=mhee The full volume can be purchased from iTunes, Amazon and other digital stores. They are read for you by Richard Mitchley & Ghizela Rowe

The Dream Woman By Wilkie Collins

THE FIRST NARRATIVE

INTRODUCTORY STATEMENT OF THE FACTS BY PERCY FAIRBANK

I

"Hullo, there! Hostler! Hullo-o-o!"

"My dear! why don't you look for the bell?"

"I HAVE looked there is no bell."

"And nobody in the yard. How very extraordinary! Call again, dear."

"Hostler! Hullo, there! Hostler-r-r!"

My second call echoes through empty space, and rouses nobody, produces, in short, no visible result. I am at the end of my resources, I don't know what to say or what to do next. Here I stand in the solitary inn yard of a strange town, with two horses to hold, and a lady to take care of. By way of adding to my responsibilities, it so happens that one of the horses is dead lame, and that the lady is my wife.

Who am I? - you will ask.

There is plenty of time to answer the question. Nothing happens; and nobody appears to receive us. Let me introduce myself and my wife.

I am Percy Fairbank, English gentleman, age (let us say) forty, no profession, moderate politics, middle height, fair complexion, easy character, plenty of money.

My wife is a French lady. She was Mademoiselle Clotilde Delorge when I was first presented to her at her father's house in France. I fell in love with her, I really don't know why. It might have been because I was perfectly idle, and had nothing else to do at the time. Or it might have been because all my friends said she was the very last woman whom I ought to think of marrying. On the surface, I must own, there is nothing in common between Mrs. Fairbank and me. She is tall; she is dark; she is nervous, excitable, romantic; in all her opinions she proceeds to extremes. What could such a woman see in me? what could I see in her? I know no more than you do. In some mysterious manner we exactly suit each other. We have been man and wife for ten years, and our only regret is, that we have no children. I don't know what YOU may think; I call that, upon the whole, a happy marriage.

So much for ourselves. The next question is - what has brought us into the inn yard? and why am I obliged to turn groom, and hold the horses?

We live for the most part in France at the country house in which my wife and I first met. Occasionally, by way of variety, we pay visits to my friends in England. We are paying one of those visits now. Our host is an old college friend of mine, possessed of a fine estate in Somersetshire; and we have arrived at his house, called Farleigh Hall toward the close of the hunting season.

On the day of which I am now writing, destined to be a memorable day in our calendar, the hounds meet at Farleigh Hall. Mrs. Fairbank and I are mounted on two of the best horses in my friend's stables. We are quite unworthy of that distinction; for we know nothing and care nothing about hunting. On the other hand, we delight in riding, and we enjoy the breezy Spring morning and the fair and fertile English landscape surrounding us on every side. While the hunt prospers, we follow the hunt. But when a check occurs, when time passes and patience is sorely tried; when the bewildered dogs run hither and thither, and strong language falls from the lips of exasperated sportsmen we fail to take any further interest in the proceedings. We turn our horses' heads in the direction of a grassy lane, delightfully shaded by trees. We trot merrily along the lane, and find ourselves on an open common.

We gallop across the common, and follow the windings of a second lane. We cross a brook, we pass through a village, we emerge into pastoral solitude among the hills. The horses toss their heads, and neigh to each other, and enjoy it as much as we do. The hunt is forgotten. We are as happy as a couple of children; we are actually singing a French song when in one moment our merriment comes to an end. My wife's horse sets one of his forefeet on a loose stone, and stumbles. His rider's ready hand saves him from falling. But, at the first attempt he makes to go on, the sad truth shows itself - a tendon is strained; the horse is lame.

What is to be done? We are strangers in a lonely part of the country. Look where we may, we see no signs of a human habitation. There is nothing for it but to take the bridle road up the hill, and try what we can discover on the other side. I transfer the saddles, and mount my wife on my own horse. He is not used to carry a lady; he misses the familiar pressure of a man's legs on either side of him; he fidgets, and starts, and kicks up the dust. I follow on foot, at a respectful distance from his heels, leading the lame horse. Is there a more miserable object on the face of creation than a lame horse? I have seen lame men and lame dogs who were cheerful creatures; but I never yet saw a lame horse who didn't look heartbroken over his own misfortune.

For half an hour my wife capers and curvets sideways along the bridle road. I trudge on behind her; and the heartbroken horse halts behind me. Hard by the top of the hill, our melancholy procession passes a Somersetshire peasant at work in a field. I summon the man to approach us; and the man looks at me stolidly, from the middle of the field, without stirring a step. I ask at the top of my voice how far it is to Farleigh Hall. The Somersetshire peasant answers at the top of HIS voice:

"Vourteen mile. Gi' oi a drap o' zyder."

I translate (for my wife's benefit) from the Somersetshire language into the English language. We are fourteen miles from Farleigh Hall; and our friend in the field desires to be rewarded, for giving us that information, with a drop of cider. There is the peasant, painted by himself! Quite a bit of character, my dear! Quite a bit of character!

Mrs. Fairbank doesn't view the study of agricultural human nature with my relish. Her fidgety horse will not allow her a moment's repose; she is beginning to lose her temper.

"We can't go fourteen miles in this way," she says. "Where is the nearest inn? Ask that brute in the field!"

I take a shilling from my pocket and hold it up in the sun. The shilling exercises magnetic virtues. The shilling draws the peasant slowly toward me from the middle of the field. I inform him that we want to put up the horses and to hire a carriage to take us back to Farleigh Hall. Where can we do that? The peasant answers (with his eye on the shilling):

"At Oonderbridge, to be zure." (At Underbridge, to be sure.)

"Is it far to Underbridge?"

The peasant repeats, "Var to Oonderbridge?" and laughs at the question. "Hoo-hoo-hoo!" (Underbridge is evidently close by, if we could only find it.) "Will you show us the way, my man?" "Will you gi' oi a drap of zyder?" I courteously bend my head, and point to the shilling. The agricultural intelligence exerts itself. The peasant joins our melancholy procession. My wife is a fine woman, but he never once looks at my wife and, more extraordinary still, he never even looks at the horses. His eyes are with his mind and his mind is on the shilling.

We reach the top of the hill and, behold on the other side, nestling in a valley, the shrine of our pilgrimage, the town of Underbridge! Here our guide claims his shilling, and leaves us to find out the inn for ourselves. I am constitutionally a polite man. I say "Good morning" at parting. The guide looks at me with the shilling between his teeth to make sure that it is a good one. "Marnin!" he says savagely and turns his back on us, as if we had offended him. A curious product, this, of the growth of civilization. If I didn't see a church spire at Underbridge, I might suppose that we had lost ourselves on a savage island.

II

Arriving at the town, we had no difficulty in finding the inn. The town is composed of one desolate street; and midway in that street stands the inn, an ancient stone building sadly out of repair. The painting on the sign-board is obliterated. The shutters over the long range of front windows are all closed. A cock and his hens are the only living creatures at the door. Plainly, this is one of the old inns of the stage-coach period, ruined by the railway. We pass through the open arched doorway, and find no one to welcome us. We advance into the stable yard behind; I assist my wife to dismount and there we are in the position already disclosed to view at the opening of this narrative. No bell to ring. No human creature to answer when I call. I stand helpless, with the bridles of the horses in my hand. Mrs. Fairbank saunters gracefully down the length of the yard and does what all women do, when they find themselves in a strange place. She opens every door as she passes it, and peeps in. On my side, I have just recovered my breath, I am on the point of shouting for the hostler for the third and last time, when I hear Mrs. Fairbank suddenly call to me:

"Percy! come here!"

Her voice is eager and agitated. She has opened a last door at the end of the yard, and has started back from some sight which has suddenly met her view. I hitch the horses' bridles on a rusty nail in the wall near me, and join my wife. She has turned pale, and catches me nervously by the arm.

"Good heavens!" she cries; "look at that!"

I look and what do I see? I see a dingy little stable, containing two stalls. In one stall a horse is munching his corn. In the other a man is lying asleep on the litter.

A worn, withered, woebegone man in a hostler's dress. His hollow wrinkled cheeks, his scanty grizzled hair, his dry yellow skin, tell their own tale of past sorrow or suffering. There is an ominous frown on his eyebrows, there is a painful nervous contraction on the side of his mouth. I hear him breathing convulsively when I first look in; he shudders and sighs in his sleep. It is not a pleasant sight to see, and I turn round instinctively to the bright sunlight in the yard. My wife turns me back again in the direction of the stable door.

"Wait!" she says. "Wait! he may do it again."

"Do what again?"

"He was talking in his sleep, Percy, when I first looked in. He was dreaming some dreadful dream. Hush! he's beginning again."

I look and listen. The man stirs on his miserable bed. The man speaks in a quick, fierce whisper through his clinched teeth. "Wake up! Wake up, there! Murder!"

There is an interval of silence. He moves one lean arm slowly until it rests over his throat; he shudders, and turns on his straw; he raises his arm from his throat, and feebly stretches it out; his hand clutches at the straw on the side toward which he has turned; he seems to fancy that he is grasping at the edge of something. I see his lips begin to move again; I step softly into the stable; my wife follows me, with her hand fast clasped in mine. We both bend over him. He is talking once more in his sleep - strange talk, mad talk, this time.

"Light gray eyes" (we hear him say), "and a droop in the left eyelid, flaxen hair, with a gold-yellow streak in it - all right, mother! fair, white arms with a down on them, little, lady's hand, with a reddish look round the fingernails, the knife, the cursed knife, first on one side, then on the other aha, you she-devil! where is the knife?"

He stops and grows restless on a sudden. We see him writhing on the straw. He throws up both his hands and gasps hysterically for breath. His eyes open suddenly. For a moment they look at nothing, with a vacant glitter in them, then they close again in deeper sleep. Is he dreaming still? Yes; but the dream seems to have taken a new course. When he speaks next, the tone is altered; the words are few - sadly and imploringly repeated over and over again. "Say you love me! I am so fond of YOU. Say you love me! say you love me!" He sinks into deeper and deeper sleep, faintly repeating those words. They die away on his lips. He speaks no more.

By this time Mrs. Fairbank has got over her terror; she is devoured by curiosity now. The miserable creature on the straw has appealed to the imaginative side of her character. Her illimitable appetite for romance hungers and thirsts for more. She shakes me impatiently by the arm.

"Do you hear? There is a woman at the bottom of it, Percy! There is love and murder in it, Percy! Where are the people of the inn? Go into the yard, and call to them again."

My wife belongs, on her mother's side, to the South of France. The South of France breeds fine women with hot tempers. I say no more. Married men will understand my position. Single men may need to be told that there are occasions when we must not only love and honor, we must also obey, our wives.

I turn to the door to obey MY wife, and find myself confronted by a stranger who has stolen on us unawares. The stranger is a tiny, sleepy, rosy old man, with a vacant pudding-face, and a shining bald head. He wears drab breeches and gaiters, and a respectable square-tailed ancient black coat. I feel instinctively that here is the landlord of the inn.

"Good morning, sir," says the rosy old man. "I'm a little hard of hearing. Was it you that was a-calling just now in the yard?"

Before I can answer, my wife interposes. She insists (in a shrill voice, adapted to our host's hardness of hearing) on knowing who that unfortunate person is sleeping on the straw. "Where does he come from? Why does he say such dreadful things in his sleep? Is he married or single? Did he ever fall in love with a murderess? What sort of a looking woman was she? Did she really stab him or not? In short, dear Mr. Landlord, tell us the whole story!"

Dear Mr. Landlord waits drowsily until Mrs. Fairbank has quite done, then delivers himself of his reply as follows:

"His name's Francis Raven. He's an Independent Methodist. He was forty-five year old last birthday. And he's my hostler. That's his story."

My wife's hot southern temper finds its way to her foot, and expresses itself by a stamp on the stable yard.

The landlord turns himself sleepily round, and looks at the horses. "A fine pair of horses, them two in the yard. Do you want to put 'em in my stables?" I reply in the affirmative by a nod. The landlord, bent on making himself agreeable to my wife, addresses her once more. "I'm a-going to wake Francis Raven. He's an Independent Methodist. He was forty-five year old last birthday. And he's my hostler. That's his story."

Having issued this second edition of his interesting narrative, the landlord enters the stable. We follow him to see how he will wake Francis Raven, and what will happen upon that. The stable broom stands in a corner; the landlord takes it, advances toward the sleeping hostler and coolly stirs the man up with a broom as if he was a wild beast in a cage. Francis Raven starts to his feet with a cry of terror - looks at us wildly, with a horrid glare of suspicion in his eyes, recovers himself the next moment and suddenly changes into a decent, quiet, respectable serving-man.

"I beg your pardon, ma'am. I beg your pardon, sir."

The tone and manner in which he makes his apologies are both above his apparent station in life. I begin to catch the infection of Mrs. Fairbank's interest in this man. We both follow him out into the yard to see what he will do with the horses. The manner in which he lifts the injured leg of the lame horse tells me at once that he understands his business. Quickly and quietly, he leads the animal into an empty stable; quickly and quietly, he gets a bucket of hot water, and puts the lame horse's leg into it. "The warm water will reduce the swelling, sir. I will bandage the leg afterwards." All that he does is done intelligently; all that he says, he says to the purpose.

Nothing wild, nothing strange about him now. Is this the same man whom we heard talking in his sleep? the same man who woke with that cry of terror and that horrid suspicion in his eyes? I determine to try him with one or two questions.

III

"Not much to do here," I say to the hostler.

"Very little to do, sir," the hostler replies.

"Anybody staying in the house?"

"The house is quite empty, sir."

"I thought you were all dead. I could make nobody hear me."

"The landlord is very deaf, sir, and the waiter is out on an errand."

"Yes; and YOU were fast asleep in the stable. Do you often take a nap in the daytime?"

The worn face of the hostler faintly flushes. His eyes look away from my eyes for the first time. Mrs. Fairbank furtively pinches my arm. Are we on the eve of a discovery at last? I repeat my question. The man has no civil alternative but to give me an answer. The answer is given in these words:

"I was tired out, sir. You wouldn't have found me asleep in the daytime but for that."

"Tired out, eh? You had been hard at work, I suppose?"

"No, sir."

"What was it, then?"

He hesitates again, and answers unwillingly, "I was up all night."

"Up all night? Anything going on in the town?"

"Nothing going on, sir."

"Anybody ill?"

"Nobody ill, sir."

That reply is the last. Try as I may, I can extract nothing more from him. He turns away and busies himself in attending to the horse's leg. I leave the stable to speak to the landlord about the carriage which is to take us back to Farleigh Hall. Mrs. Fairbank remains with the hostler, and favors me with a look at parting. The look says plainly, "I mean to find out why he was up all night. Leave him to Me."

The ordering of the carriage is easily accomplished. The inn possesses one horse and one chaise. The landlord has a story to tell of the horse, and a story to tell of the chaise. They resemble the story of Francis Raven with this exception, that the horse and chaise belong to no religious persuasion. "The horse will be nine year old next birthday. I've had the shay for four- and-twenty year. Mr. Max, of Underbridge, he bred the horse; and Mr. Pooley, of Yeovil, he built the shay. It's my horse and my shay. And that's THEIR story!" Having relieved his mind of these details, the landlord proceeds to put the harness on the horse. By way of assisting him, I drag the chaise into the yard. Just as our preparations are completed, Mrs. Fairbank appears. A moment or two later the hostler follows her out. He has bandaged the horse's leg, and is now ready to drive us to Farleigh Hall. I observe signs of agitation in his face and manner, which suggest that my wife has found her way into his confidence. I put the question to her privately in a corner of the yard. "Well? Have you found out why Francis Raven was up all night?"

Mrs. Fairbank has an eye to dramatic effect. Instead of answering plainly, Yes or No, she suspends the interest and excites the audience by putting a question on her side.

"What is the day of the month, dear?"

"The day of the month is the first of March."

"The first of March, Percy, is Francis Raven's birthday."

I try to look as if I was interested and don't succeed.

"Francis was born," Mrs. Fairbank proceeds gravely, "at two o'clock in the morning."

I begin to wonder whether my wife's intellect is going the way of the landlord's intellect. "Is that all?" I ask.

"It is NOT all," Mrs. Fairbank answers. "Francis Raven sits up on the morning of his birthday because he is afraid to go to bed."

"And why is he afraid to go to bed?"

"Because he is in peril of his life."

"On his birthday?"

"On his birthday. At two o'clock in the morning. As regularly as the birthday comes round."

There she stops. Has she discovered no more than that? No more thus far. I begin to feel really interested by this time. I ask eagerly what it means? Mrs. Fairbank points mysteriously to the chaise with Francis Raven (hitherto our hostler, now our coachman) waiting for us to get in. The chaise has a seat for two in front, and a seat for one behind. My wife casts a warning look at me, and places herself on the seat in front.

The necessary consequence of this arrangement is that Mrs. Fairhank sits by the side of the driver during a journey of two hours and more. Need I state the result? It would be an insult to your intelligence to state the result. Let me offer you my place in the chaise. And let Francis Raven tell his terrible story in his own words.

THE SECOND NARRATIVE

THE HOSTLER'S STORY. TOLD BY HIMSELF

IV

It is now ten years ago since I got my first warning of the great trouble of my life in the Vision of a Dream.

I shall be better able to tell you about it if you will please suppose yourselves to be drinking tea along with us in our little cottage in Cambridgeshire, ten years since.

The time was the close of day, and there were three of us at the table, namely, my mother, myself, and my mother's sister, Mrs. Chance. These two were Scotchwomen by birth, and both were widows. There was no other resemblance between them that I can call to mind. My mother had lived all her life in England, and had no more of the Scotch brogue on her tongue than I have. My aunt Chance had never been out of Scotland until she came to keep house with my mother after her husband's death. And when SHE opened her lips you heard broad Scotch, I can tell you, if you ever heard it yet!

As it fell out, there was a matter of some consequence in debate among us that evening. It was this: whether I should do well or not to take a long journey on foot the next morning.

Now the next morning happened to be the day before my birthday; and the purpose of the journey was to offer myself for a situation as groom at a great house in the neighboring county to ours. The place was reported as likely to fall vacant in about three weeks' time. I was as well fitted to fill it as any other man. In the prosperous days of our family, my father had been manager of a training stable, and he had kept me employed among the horses from my boyhood upward. Please to excuse my troubling you with these small matters. They all fit into my story farther on, as you will soon find out. My poor mother was dead against my leaving home on the morrow.

"You can never walk all the way there and all the way back again by to-morrow night," she says. "The end of it will be that you will sleep away from home on your birthday. You have never done that yet, Francis, since your father's death, I don't like your doing it now. Wait a day longer, my son, only one day."

For my own part, I was weary of being idle, and I couldn't abide the notion of delay. Even one day might make all the difference. Some other man might take time by the forelock, and get the place.

"Consider how long I have been out of work," I says, "and don't ask me to put off the journey. I won't fail you, mother. I'll get back by to-morrow night, if I have to pay my last sixpence for a lift in a cart."

My mother shook her head. "I don't like it, Francis, I don't like it!" There was no moving her from that view. We argued and argued, until we were both at a deadlock. It ended in our agreeing to refer the difference between us to my mother's sister, Mrs. Chance.

While we were trying hard to convince each other, my aunt Chance sat as dumb as a fish, stirring her tea and thinking her own thoughts. When we made our appeal to her, she seemed as it were to wake up. "Ye baith refer it to my puir judgment?" she says, in her broad Scotch. We both answered Yes.

Upon that my aunt Chance first cleared the tea-table, and then pulled out from the pocket of her gown a pack of cards.

Don't run away, if you please, with the notion that this was done lightly, with a view to amuse my mother and me. My aunt Chance seriously believed that she could look into the future by telling fortunes on the cards. She did nothing herself without first consulting the cards. She could give no more serious proof of her interest in my welfare than the proof which she was offering now. I don't say it profanely; I only mention the fact the cards had, in some incomprehensible way, got themselves jumbled up together with her religious convictions. You meet with people nowadays who believe in spirits working by way of tables and chairs. On the same principle (if there IS any principle in it) my aunt Chance believed in Providence working by way of the cards.

"Whether YOU are right, Francie, or your mither, whether ye will do weel or ill, the morrow, to go or stay the cairds will tell it. We are a' in the hands of Proavidence. The cairds will tell it."

Hearing this, my mother turned her head aside, with something of a sour look in her face. Her sister's notions about the cards were little better than flat blasphemy to her mind. But she kept her opinion to herself. My aunt Chance, to own the truth, had inherited, through her late husband, a pension of thirty pounds a year. This was an important contribution to our housekeeping, and we poor relations were bound to treat her with a certain respect. As for myself, if my poor father never did anything else for me before he fell into difficulties, he gave me a good education, and raised me (thank God) above superstitions of all sorts. However, a very little amused me in those days; and I waited to have my fortune told, as patiently as if I believed in it too!

My aunt began her hocus pocus by throwing out all the cards in the pack under seven. She shuffled the rest with her left hand for luck; and then she gave them to me to cut. "Wi' yer left hand, Francie. Mind that! Pet your trust in Proavidence but dinna forget that your luck's in yer left hand!" A long and roundabout shifting of the cards followed, reducing them in number until there were just fifteen of them left, laid out neatly before my aunt in a half circle. The card which happened to lie outermost, at the right-hand end of the circle, was, according to rule in such cases, the card chosen to represent Me. By way of being appropriate to my situation as a poor groom out of employment, the card was the King of Diamonds.

"I tak' up the King o' Diamants," says my aunt. "I count seven cairds fra' richt to left; and I humbly ask a blessing on what follows." My aunt shut her eyes as if she was saying grace before meat, and held up to me the seventh card. I called the seventh card - the Queen of Spades. My aunt opened her eyes again in a hurry, and cast a sly look my way. "The Queen o' Spades means a dairk woman. Ye'll be thinking in secret, Francie, of a dairk woman?"

When a man has been out of work for more than three months, his mind isn't troubled much with thinking of women, light or dark. I was thinking of the groom's place at the great house, and I tried to say so. My aunt Chance wouldn't listen. She treated my interpretation with contempt. "Hoot-toot! there's the caird in your hand! If ye're no thinking of her the day, ye'll be thinking of her the morrow. Where's the harm of thinking of a dairk woman! I was ance a dairk woman myself, before my hair was gray. Haud yer peace, Francie, and watch the cairds."

I watched the cards as I was told. There were seven left on the table. My aunt removed two from one end of the row and two from the other, and desired me to call the two outermost of the three cards now left on the table. I called the Ace of Clubs and the Ten of Diamonds. My aunt Chance lifted her eyes to the ceiling with a look of devout gratitude which sorely tried my mother's patience. The Ace of Clubs and the Ten of Diamonds, taken together, signified, first, good news (evidently the news of the groom's place); secondly, a journey that lay before me (pointing plainly to my journey to-morrow!); thirdly and lastly, a sum of money (probably the groom's wages!) waiting to find its way into my pockets. Having told my fortune in these encouraging terms, my aunt declined to carry the experiment any further. "Eh, lad! it's a clean tempting o' Proavidence to ask mair o' the cairds than the cairds have tauld us noo. Gae yer ways to-morrow to the great hoose. A dairk woman will meet ye at the gate; and she'll have a hand in getting ye the groom's place, wi' a' the gratifications and pairquisites appertaining to the same. And, mebbe, when yer poaket's full o' money, ye'll no' be forgetting yer aunt Chance, maintaining her ain unblemished widowhood, wi' Proavidence assisting, on thratty punds a year!"

I promised to remember my aunt Chance (who had the defect, by the way, of being a terribly greedy person after money) on the next happy occasion when my poor empty pockets were to be filled at last. This done, I looked at my mother. She had agreed to take her sister for umpire between us, and her sister had given it in my favor. She raised no more objections. Silently, she got on her feet, and kissed me, and sighed bitterly and so left the room. My aunt Chance shook her head. "I doubt, Francie, yer puir mither has but a heathen notion of the vairtue of the cairds!"

By daylight the next morning I set forth on my journey. I looked back at the cottage as I opened the garden gate. At one window was my mother, with her handkerchief to her eyes. At the other stood my aunt Chance, holding up the Queen of Spades by way of encouraging me at starting. I waved my hands to both of them in token of farewell, and stepped out briskly into the road. It was then the last day of February. Be pleased to remember, in connection with this, that the first of March was the day, and two o'clock in the morning the hour of my birth.

V

Now you know how I came to leave home. The next thing to tell is, what happened on the journey.

I reached the great house in reasonably good time considering the distance. At the very first trial of it, the prophecy of the cards turned out to be wrong. The person who met me at the lodge gate was not a dark woman in fact, not a woman at all but a boy. He directed me on the way to the servants' offices; and there again the cards were all wrong. I encountered, not one woman, but three and not one of the three was dark. I have stated that I am not superstitious, and I have told the truth. But I must own that I did feel a certain fluttering at the heart when I made my bow to the steward, and told him what business had brought me to the house. His answer completed the discomfiture of aunt Chance's fortune-telling. My ill-luck still pursued me. That very morning another man had applied for the groom's place, and had got it.

I swallowed my disappointment as well as I could, and thanked the steward, and went to the inn in the village to get the rest and food which I sorely needed by this time.

Before starting on my homeward walk I made some inquiries at the inn, and ascertained that I might save a few miles, on my return, by following a new road. Furnished with full instructions, several times repeated, as to the various turnings I was to take, I set forth, and walked on till the evening with only one stoppage for bread and cheese. Just as it was getting toward dark, the rain came on and the wind began to rise; and I found myself, to make matters worse, in a part of the country with which I was entirely unacquainted, though I guessed myself to be some fifteen miles from home. The first house I found to inquire at, was a lonely roadside inn, standing on the outskirts of a thick wood. Solitary as the place looked, it was welcome to a lost man who was also hungry, thirsty, footsore, and wet. The landlord was civil and respectable-looking; and the price he asked for a bed was reasonable enough. I was grieved to disappoint my mother. But there was no conveyance to be had, and I could go no farther afoot that night. My weariness fairly forced me to stop at the inn.

I may say for myself that I am a temperate man. My supper simply consisted of some rashers of bacon, a slice of home-made bread, and a pint of ale. I did not go to bed immediately after this moderate meal, but sat up with the landlord, talking about my bad prospects and my long run of ill-luck, and diverging from these topics to the subjects of horse-flesh and racing. Nothing was said, either by myself, my host, or the few laborers who strayed into the tap-room, which could, in the slightest degree, excite my mind, or set my fancy, which is only a small fancy at the best of times, playing tricks with my common sense.

At a little after eleven the house was closed. I went round with the landlord, and held the candle while the doors and lower windows were being secured. I noticed with surprise the strength of the bolts, bars, and iron-sheathed shutters.

"You see, we are rather lonely here," said the landlord. "We never have had any attempts to break in yet, but it's always as well to be on the safe side. When nobody is sleeping here, I am the only man in the house. My wife and daughter are timid, and the servant girl takes after her missuses. Another glass of ale, before you turn in? No! Well, how such a sober man as you comes to be out of a place is more than I can understand for one. Here's where you're to sleep. You're the only lodger to-night, and I think you'll say my missus has done her best to make you comfortable. You're quite sure you won't have another glass of ale? Very well. Good night."

It was half-past eleven by the clock in the passage as we went upstairs to the bedroom. The window looked out on the wood at the back of the house.

I locked my door, set my candle on the chest of drawers, and wearily got me ready for bed. The bleak wind was still blowing, and the solemn, surging moan of it in the wood was very dreary to hear through the night silence. Feeling strangely wakeful, I resolved to keep the candle alight until I began to grow sleepy. The truth is, I was not quite myself. I was depressed in mind by my disappointment of the morning; and I was worn out in body by my long walk. Between the two, I own I couldn't face the prospect of lying awake in the darkness, listening to the dismal moan of the wind in the wood.

Sleep stole on me before I was aware of it; my eyes closed, and I fell off to rest, without having so much as thought of extinguishing the candle.

The next thing that I remember was a faint shivering that ran through me from head to foot, and a dreadful sinking pain at my heart, such as I had never felt before. The shivering only disturbed my slumbers; the pain woke me instantly. In one moment I passed from a state of sleep to a state of wakefulness, my eyes wide open, my mind clear on a sudden as if by a miracle. The candle had burned down nearly to the last morsel of tallow, but the unsnuffed wick had just fallen off, and the light was, for the moment, fair and full.

Between the foot of the bed and the closet door, I saw a person in my room. The person was a woman, standing looking at me, with a knife in her hand. It does no credit to my courage to confess it but the truth IS the truth. I was struck speechless with terror. There I lay with my eyes on the woman; there the woman stood (with the knife in her hand) with HER eyes on ME.

She said not a word as we stared each other in the face; but she moved after a little, moved slowly toward the left-hand side of the bed.

The light fell full on her face. A fair, fine woman, with yellowish flaxen hair, and light gray eyes, with a droop in the left eyelid. I noticed these things and fixed them in my mind, before she was quite round at the side of the bed. Without saying a word; without any change in the stony stillness of her face; without any noise following her footfall, she came closer and closer; stopped at the bed-head; and lifted the knife to stab me. I laid my arm over my throat to save it; but, as I saw the blow coming, I threw my hand across the bed to the right side, and jerked my body over that way, just as the knife came down, like lightning, within a hair's breadth of my shoulder.

My eyes fixed on her arm and her hand, she gave me time to look at them as she slowly drew the knife out of the bed. A white, well-shaped arm, with a pretty down lying lightly over the fair skin. A delicate lady's hand, with a pink flush round the finger nails.

She drew the knife out, and passed back again slowly to the foot of the bed; she stopped there for a moment looking at me; then she came on without saying a word; without any change in the stony stillness of her face; without any noise following her footfall came on to the side of the bed where I now lay.

Getting near me, she lifted the knife again, and I drew myself away to the left side. She struck, as before right into the mattress, with a swift downward action of her arm; and she missed me, as before; by a hair's breadth. This time my eyes wandered from HER to the knife. It was like the large clasp knives which laboring men use to cut their bread and bacon with. Her delicate little fingers did not hide more than two thirds of the handle; I noticed that it was made of buckhorn, clean and shining as the blade was, and looking like new.

For the second time she drew the knife out of the bed, and suddenly hid it away in the wide sleeve of her gown. That done, she stopped by the bedside watching me. For an instant I saw her standing in that position, then the wick of the spent candle fell over into the socket. The flame dwindled to a little blue point, and the room grew dark.

A moment, or less, if possible, passed so and then the wick flared up, smokily, for the last time. My eyes were still looking for her over the right-hand side of the bed when the last flash of light came. Look as I might, I could see nothing. The woman with the knife was gone.

I began to get back to myself again. I could feel my heart beating; I could hear the woeful moaning of the wind in the wood; I could leap up in bed, and give the alarm before she escaped from the house. "Murder! Wake up there! Murder!"

Nobody answered to the alarm. I rose and groped my way through the darkness to the door of the room. By that way she must have got in. By that way she must have gone out.

The door of the room was fast locked, exactly as I had left it on going to bed! I looked at the window. Fast locked too!

Hearing a voice outside, I opened the door. There was the landlord, coming toward me along the passage, with his burning candle in one hand, and his gun in the other.

"What is it?" he says, looking at me in no very friendly way.

I could only answer in a whisper, "A woman, with a knife in her hand. In my room. A fair, yellow-haired woman. She jabbed at me with the knife, twice over."

He lifted his candle, and looked at me steadily from head to foot. "She seems to have missed you - twice over."

"I dodged the knife as it came down. It struck the bed each time. Go in, and see."

The landlord took his candle into the bedroom immediately. In less than a minute he came out again into the passage in a violent passion.

"The devil fly away with you and your woman with the knife! There isn't a mark in the bedclothes anywhere. What do you mean by coming into a man's place and frightening his family out of their wits by a dream?"

A dream? The woman who had tried to stab me, not a living human being like myself? I began to shake and shiver. The horrors got hold of me at the bare thought of it.

"I'll leave the house," I said. "Better be out on the road in the rain and dark, than back in that room, after what I've seen in it. Lend me the light to get my clothes by, and tell me what I'm to pay."

The landlord led the way back with his light into the bedroom. "Pay?" says he. "You'll find your score on the slate when you go downstairs. I wouldn't have taken you in for all the money you've got about you, if I had known your dreaming, screeching ways beforehand. Look at the bed, where's the cut of a knife in it? Look at the window, is the lock bursted? Look at the door (which I heard you fasten yourself) is it broke in? A murdering woman with a knife in my house! You ought to be ashamed of yourself!"

My eyes followed his hand as it pointed first to the bed, then to the window, then to the door. There was no gainsaying it. The bed sheet was as sound as on the day it was made. The window was fast. The door hung on its hinges as steady as ever. I huddled my clothes on without speaking. We went downstairs together. I looked at the clock in the bar-room. The time was twenty minutes past two in the morning. I paid my bill, and the landlord let me out. The rain had ceased; but the night was dark, and the wind was bleaker than ever. Little did the darkness, or the cold, or the doubt about the way home matter to ME. My mind was away from all these things. My mind was fixed on the vision in the bedroom. What had I seen trying to murder me? The creature of a dream? Or that other creature from the world beyond the grave, whom men call ghost? I could make nothing of it as I walked along in the night; I had made nothing by it by midday when I stood at last, after many times missing my road, on the doorstep of home.

VI

My mother came out alone to welcome me back. There were no secrets between us two. I told her all that had happened, just as I have told it to you. She kept silence till I had done. And then she put a question to me.

"What time was it, Francis, when you saw the Woman in your Dream?"

I had looked at the clock when I left the inn, and I had noticed that the hands pointed to twenty minutes past two. Allowing for the time consumed in speaking to the landlord, and in getting on my clothes, I answered that I must have first seen the Woman at two o'clock in the morning. In other words, I had not only seen her on my birthday, but at the hour of my birth.

My mother still kept silence. Lost in her own thoughts, she took me by the hand, and led me into the parlor. Her writing-desk was on the table by the fireplace. She opened it, and signed to me to take a chair by her side.

"My son! your memory is a bad one, and mine is fast failing me. Tell me again what the Woman looked like. I want her to be as well known to both of us, years hence, as she is now."

I obeyed; wondering what strange fancy might be working in her mind. I spoke; and she wrote the words as they fell from my lips:

"Light gray eyes, with a droop in the left eyelid. Flaxen hair, with a golden-yellow streak in it. White arms, with a down upon them. Little, lady's hands, with a rosy-red look about the finger nails."

"Did you notice how she was dressed, Francis?"

"No, mother."

"Did you notice the knife?"

"Yes. A large clasp knife, with a buckhorn handle, as good as new."

My mother added the description of the knife. Also the year, month, day of the week, and hour of the day when the Dream-Woman appeared to me at the inn. That done, she locked up the paper in her desk.

"Not a word, Francis, to your aunt. Not a word to any living soul. Keep your Dream a secret between you and me."

The weeks passed, and the months passed. My mother never returned to the subject again. As for me, time, which wears out all things, wore out my remembrance of the Dream. Little by little, the image of the Woman grew dimmer and dimmer. Little by little, she faded out of my mind.

VII

The story of the warning is now told. Judge for yourself if it was a true warning or a false, when you hear what happened to me on my next birthday.

In the Summer time of the year, the Wheel of Fortune turned the right way for me at last. I was smoking my pipe one day, near an old stone quarry at the entrance to our village, when a carriage accident happened, which gave a new turn, as it were, to my lot in life. It was an accident of the commonest kind not worth mentioning at any length. A lady driving herself; a runaway horse; a cowardly man-servant in attendance, frightened out of his wits; and the stone quarry too near to be agreeable, that is what I saw, all in a few moments, between two whiffs of my pipe. I stopped the horse at the edge of the quarry, and got myself a little hurt by the shaft of the chaise. But that didn't matter. The lady declared I had saved her life; and her husband, coming with her to our cottage the next day, took me into his service then and there. The lady happened to be of a dark complexion; and it may amuse you to hear that my aunt Chance instantly pitched on that circumstance as a means of saving the credit of the cards. Here was the promise of the Queen of Spades performed to the very letter, by means of "a dark woman," just as my aunt had told me. "In the time to come, Francis, beware o' pettin' yer ain blinded intairpretation on the cairds. Ye're ower ready, I trow, to murmur under dispensation of Proavidence that ye canna fathom like the Eesraelites of auld. I'll say nae mair to ye. Mebbe when the mony's powering into yer poakets, ye'll no forget yer aunt Chance, left like a sparrow on the housetop, wi a sma' annuitee o' thratty punds a year."

I remained in my situation (at the West-end of London) until the Spring of the New Year. About that time, my master's health failed. The doctors ordered him away to foreign parts, and the establishment was broken up. But the turn in my luck still held good. When I left my place, I left it - thanks to the generosity of my kind master with a yearly allowance granted to me, in remembrance of the day when I had saved my mistress's life. For the future, I could go back to service or not, as I pleased; my little income was enough to support my mother and myself.

My master and mistress left England toward the end of February. Certain matters of business to do for them detained me in London until the last day of the month. I was only able to leave for our village by the evening train, to keep my birthday with my mother as usual. It was bedtime when I got to the cottage; and I was sorry to find that she was far from well. To make matters worse, she had finished her bottle of medicine on the previous day, and had omitted to get it replenished, as the doctor had strictly directed. He dispensed his own medicines, and I offered to go and knock him up. She refused to let me do this; and, after giving me my supper, sent me away to my bed.

I fell asleep for a little, and woke again. My mother's bed- chamber was next to mine. I heard my aunt Chance's heavy footsteps going to and fro in the room, and, suspecting something wrong, knocked at the door. My mother's pains had returned upon her; there was a serious necessity for relieving her sufferings as speedily as possible, I put on my clothes, and ran off, with the medicine bottle in my hand, to the other end of the village, where the doctor lived. The church clock chimed the quarter to two on my birthday just as I reached his house. One ring of the night bell brought him to his bedroom window to speak to me. He told me to wait, and he would let me in at the surgery door. I noticed, while I was waiting, that the night was wonderfully fair and warm for the time of year. The old stone quarry where the carriage accident had happened was within view. The moon in the clear heavens lit it up almost as bright as day.

In a minute or two the doctor let me into the surgery. I closed the door, noticing that he had left his room very lightly clad. He kindly pardoned my mother's neglect of his directions, and set to work at once at compounding the medicine. We were both intent on the bottle; he filling it, and I holding the light when we heard the surgery door suddenly opened from the street.

VIII

Who could possibly be up and about in our quiet village at the second hour of the morning?

The person who opened the door appeared within range of the light of the candle. To complete our amazement, the person proved to be a woman! She walked up to the counter, and standing side by side with me, lifted her veil. At the moment when she showed her face, I heard the church clock strike two. She was a stranger to me, and a stranger to the doctor. She was also, beyond all comparison, the most beautiful woman I have ever seen in my life.

"I saw the light under the door," she said. "I want some medicine."

She spoke quite composedly, as if there was nothing at all extraordinary in her being out in the village at two in the morning, and following me into the surgery to ask for medicine! The doctor stared at her as if he suspected his own eyes of deceiving him. "Who are you?" be asked. "How do you come to be wandering about at this time in the morning?"

She paid no heed to his questions. She only told him coolly what she wanted. "I have got a bad toothache. I want a bottle of laudanum."

The doctor recovered himself when she asked for the laudanum. He was on his own ground, you know, when it came to a matter of laudanum; and he spoke to her smartly enough this time.

"Oh, you have got the toothache, have you? Let me look at the tooth."

She shook her bead, and laid a two-shilling piece on the counter. "I won't trouble you to look at the tooth," she said. "There is the money. Let me have the laudanum, if you please."

The doctor put the two-shilling piece back again in her hand. "I don't sell laudanum to strangers," he answered. "If you are in any distress of body or mind, that is another matter. I shall be glad to help you."

She put the money back in her pocket. "YOU can't help me," she said, as quietly as ever. "Good morning."

With that, she opened the surgery door to go out again into the street. So far, I had not spoken a word on my side. I had stood with the candle in my hand (not knowing I was holding it) with my eyes fixed on her, with my mind fixed on her like a man bewitched. Her looks betrayed, even more plainly than her words, her resolution, in one way or another, to destroy herself. When she opened the door, in my alarm at what might happen I found the use of my tongue.

"Stop!" I cried out. "Wait for me. I want to speak to you before you go away." She lifted her eyes with a look of careless surprise and a mocking smile on her lips.

"What can YOU have to say to me?" She stopped, and laughed to herself. "Why not?" she said. "I have got nothing to do, and nowhere to go." She turned back a step, and nodded to me. "You're a strange man, I think I'll humor you, I'll wait outside." The door of the surgery closed on her. She was gone.

I am ashamed to own what happened next. The only excuse for me is that I was really and truly a man bewitched. I turned me round to follow her out, without once thinking of my mother. The doctor stopped me.

"Don't forget the medicine," he said. "And if you will take my advice, don't trouble yourself about that woman. Rouse up the constable. It's his business to look after her, not yours."

I held out my hand for the medicine in silence: I was afraid I should fail in respect if I trusted myself to answer him. He must have seen, as I saw, that she wanted the laudanum to poison herself. He had, to my mind, taken a very heartless view of the matter. I just thanked him when he gave me the medicine and went out.

She was waiting for me as she had promised; walking slowly to and fro, a tall, graceful, solitary figure in the bright moonbeams. They shed over her fair complexion, her bright golden hair, her large gray eyes, just the light that suited them best. She looked hardly mortal when she first turned to speak to me.

"Well?" she said. "And what do you want?"

In spite of my pride, or my shyness, or my better sense, whichever it might be, all my heart went out to her in a moment. I caught hold of her by the hands, and owned what was in my thoughts, as freely as if I had known her for half a lifetime.

"You mean to destroy yourself," I said. "And I mean to prevent you from doing it. If I follow you about all night, I'll prevent you from doing it."

She laughed. "You saw yourself that he wouldn't sell me the laudanum. Do you really care whether I live or die?" She squeezed my hands gently as she put the question: her eyes searched mine with a languid, lingering look in them that ran through me like fire. My voice died away on my lips; I couldn't answer her.

She understood, without my answering. "You have given me a fancy for living, by speaking kindly to me," she said. "Kindness has a wonderful effect on women, and dogs, and other domestic animals. It is only men who are superior to kindness. Make your mind easy - I promise to take as much care of myself as if I was the happiest woman living! Don't let me keep you here, out of your bed. Which way are you going?"

Miserable wretch that I was, I had forgotten my mother with the medicine in my hand! "I am going home," I said. "Where are you staying? At the inn?"

She laughed her bitter laugh, and pointed to the stone quarry. "There is MY inn for to-night," she said. "When I got tired of walking about, I rested there."

We walked on together, on my way home. I took the liberty of asking her if she had any friends.

"I thought I had one friend left," she said, "or you would never have met me in this place. It turns out I was wrong. My friend's door was closed in my face some hours since; my friend's servants threatened me with the police. I had nowhere else to go, after trying my luck in your neighborhood; and nothing left but my two- shilling piece and these rags on my back. What respectable innkeeper would take ME into his house? I walked about, wondering how I could find my way out of the world without disfiguring myself, and without suffering much pain. You have no river in these parts. I didn't see my way out of the world, till I heard you ringing at the doctor's house. I got a glimpse at the bottles in the surgery, when he let you in, and I thought of the laudanum directly. What were you doing there? Who is that medicine for? Your wife?"

"I am not married!"

She laughed again. "Not married! If I was a little better dressed there might be a chance for ME. Where do you live? Here?"

We had arrived, by this time, at my mother's door. She held out her hand to say good-by. Houseless and homeless as she was, she never asked me to give her a shelter for the night. It was MY proposal that she should rest, under my roof, unknown to my mother and my aunt. Our kitchen was built out at the back of the cottage: she might remain there unseen and unheard until the household was astir in the morning. I led her into the kitchen, and set a chair for her by the dying embers of the fire. I dare say I was to blame, shamefully to blame, if you like. I only wonder what YOU would have done in my place. On your word of honor as a man, would YOU have let that beautiful creature wander back to the shelter of the stone quarry like a stray dog? God help the woman who is foolish enough to trust and love you, if you would have done that!

I left her by the fire, and went to my mother's room.

IX

If you have ever felt the heartache, you will know what I suffered in secret when my mother took my hand, and said, "I am sorry, Francis, that your night's rest has been disturbed through ME." I gave her the medicine; and I waited by her till the pains abated. My aunt Chance went back to her bed; and my mother and I were left alone. I noticed that her writing-desk, moved from its customary place, was on the bed by her side. She saw me looking at it. "This is your birthday, Francis," she said. "Have you anything to tell me?" I had so completely forgotten my Dream, that I had no notion of what was passing in her mind when she said those words. For a moment there was a guilty fear in me that she suspected something. I turned away my face, and said, "No, mother; I have nothing to tell." She signed to me to stoop down over the pillow and kiss her. "God bless you, my love!" she said; and many happy returns of the day." She patted my hand, and closed her weary eyes, and, little by little, fell off peaceably into sleep.

I stole downstairs again. I think the good influence of my mother must have followed me down. At any rate, this is true: I stopped with my hand on the closed kitchen door, and said to myself: "Suppose I leave the house, and leave the village, without seeing her or speaking to her more?"

Should I really have fled from temptation in this way, if I had been left to myself to decide? Who can tell? As things were, I was not left to decide. While my doubt was in my mind, she heard me, and opened the kitchen door. My eyes and her eyes met. That ended it.

We were together, unsuspected and undisturbed, for the next two hours. Time enough for her to reveal the secret of her wasted life. Time enough for her to take possession of me as her own, to do with me as she liked. It is needless to dwell here on the misfortunes which had brought her low; they are misfortunes too common to interest anybody.

Her name was Alicia Warlock. She had been born and bred a lady. She had lost her station, her character, and her friends. Virtue shuddered at the sight of her; and Vice had got her for the rest of her days. Shocking and common, as I told you. It made no difference to ME. I have said it already, I say it again, I was a man bewitched. Is there anything so very wonderful in that? Just remember who I was. Among the honest women in my own station in life, where could I have found the like of HER? Could THEY walk as she walked? and look as she looked? When THEY gave me a kiss, did their lips linger over it as hers did? Had THEY her skin, her laugh, her foot, her hand, her touch? SHE never had a speck of dirt on her: I tell you her flesh was a perfume. When she embraced me, her arms folded round me like the wings of angels; and her smile covered me softly with its light like the sun in heaven. I leave you to laugh at me, or to cry over me, just as your temper may incline. I am not trying to excuse myself I am trying to explain. You are gentle-folks; what dazzled and maddened ME, is everyday experience to YOU. Fallen or not, angel or devil, it came to this, she was a lady; and I was a groom.

Before the house was astir, I got her away (by the workmen's train) to a large manufacturing town in our parts.

Here, with my savings in money to help her, she could get her outfit of decent clothes and her lodging among strangers who asked no questions so long as they were paid. Here, now on one pretense and now on another, I could visit her, and we could both plan together what our future lives were to be. I need not tell you that I stood pledged to make her my wife. A man in my station always marries a woman of her sort.

Do you wonder if I was happy at this time? I should have been perfectly happy but for one little drawback. It was this: I was never quite at my ease in the presence of my promised wife.

I don't mean that I was shy with her, or suspicious of her, or ashamed of her. The uneasiness I am speaking of was caused by a faint doubt in my mind whether I had not seen her somewhere, before the morning when we met at the doctor's house. Over and over again, I found myself wondering whether her face did not remind me of some other face, what other I never could tell. This strange feeling, this one question that could never be answered, vexed me to a degree that you would hardly credit. It came between us at the strangest times oftenest, however, at night, when the candles were lit. You have known what it is to try and remember a forgotten name and to fail, search as you may, to find it in your mind. That was my case. I failed to find my lost face, just as you failed to find your lost name.

In three weeks we had talked matters over, and had arranged how I was to make a clean breast of it at home. By Alicia's advice, I was to describe her as having been one of my fellow servants during the time I was employed under my kind master and mistress in London. There was no fear now of my mother taking any harm from the shock of a great surprise. Her health had improved during the three weeks' interval. On the first evening when she was able to take her old place at tea time, I summoned my courage, and told her I was going to be married. The poor soul flung her arms round my neck, and burst out crying for joy. "Oh, Francis!" she says, "I am so glad you will have somebody to comfort you and care for you when I am gone!" As for my aunt Chance, you can anticipate what SHE did, without being told. Ah, me! If there had really been any prophetic virtue in the cards, what a terrible warning they might have given us that night! It was arranged that I was to bring my promised wife to dinner at the cottage on the next day.

X

I own I was proud of Alicia when I led her into our little parlor at the appointed time. She had never, to my mind, looked so beautiful as she looked that day. I never noticed any other woman's dress, I noticed hers as carefully as if I had been a woman myself! She wore a black silk gown, with plain collar and cuffs, and a modest lavender-colored bonnet, with one white rose in it placed at the side. My mother, dressed in her Sunday best, rose up, all in a flutter, to welcome her daughter-in-law that was to be. She walked forward a few steps, half smiling, half in tears, she looked Alicia full in the face and suddenly stood still. Her cheeks turned white in an instant; her eyes stared in horror; her hands dropped helplessly at her sides. She staggered back, and fell into the arms of my aunt, standing behind her. It was no swoon, she kept her senses. Her eyes turned slowly from Alicia to me. "Francis," she said, "does that woman's face remind you of nothing?"

Before I could answer, she pointed to her writing-desk on the table at the fireside. "Bring it!" she cried, "bring it!"

At the same moment I felt Alicia's hand on my shoulder, and saw Alicia's face red with anger and no wonder!

"What does this mean?" she asked. "Does your mother want to insult me?"

I said a few words to quiet her; what they were I don't remember, I was so confused and astonished at the time. Before I had done, I heard my mother behind me.

My aunt had fetched her desk. She had opened it; she had taken a paper from it. Step by step, helping herself along by the wall, she came nearer and nearer, with the paper in her hand. She looked at the paper, she looked in Alicia's face, she lifted the long, loose sleeve of her gown, and examined her hand and arm. I saw fear suddenly take the place of anger in Alicia's eyes. She shook herself free of my mother's grasp. "Mad!" she said to herself, "and Francis never told me!" With those words she ran out of the room.

I was hastening out after her, when my mother signed to me to stop. She read the words written on the paper. While they fell slowly, one by one, from her lips, she pointed toward the open door.

"Light gray eyes, with a droop in the left eyelid. Flaxen hair, with a gold-yellow streak in it. White arms, with a down upon them. Little, lady's hand, with a rosy-red look about the finger nails. The Dream Woman, Francis! The Dream Woman!"

Something darkened the parlor window as those words were spoken. I looked sidelong at the shadow. Alicia Warlock had come back! She was peering in at us over the low window blind. There was the fatal face which had first looked at me in the bedroom of the lonely inn. There, resting on the window blind, was the lovely little hand which had held the murderous knife. I HAD seen her before we met in the village. The Dream Woman! The Dream Woman!

XI

I expect nobody to approve of what I have next to tell of myself. In three weeks from the day when my mother had identified her with the Woman of the Dream, I took Alicia Warlock to church, and made her my wife. I was a man bewitched. Again and again I say it - I was a man bewitched!

During the interval before my marriage, our little household at the cottage was broken up. My mother and my aunt quarreled. My mother, believing in the Dream, entreated me to break off my engagement. My aunt, believing in the cards, urged me to marry.

This difference of opinion produced a dispute between them, in the course of which my aunt Chance, quite unconscious of having any superstitious feelings of her own, actually set out the cards which prophesied happiness to me in my married life, and asked my mother how anybody but "a blinded heathen could be fule enough, after seeing those cairds, to believe in a dream!" This was, naturally, too much for my mother's patience; hard words followed on either side; Mrs. Chance returned in dudgeon to her friends in Scotland. She left me a written statement of my future prospects, as revealed by the cards, and with it an address at which a post-office order would reach her. "The day was not that far off," she remarked, "when Francie might remember what he owed to his aunt Chance, maintaining her ain unbleemished widowhood on thratty punds a year."

Having refused to give her sanction to my marriage, my mother also refused to be present at the wedding, or to visit Alicia afterwards. There was no anger at the bottom of this conduct on her part. Believing as she did in this Dream, she was simply in mortal fear of my wife. I understood this, and I made allowances for her. Not a cross word passed between us. My one happy remembrance now, though I did disobey her in the matter of my marriage, is this: I loved and respected my good mother to the last.

As for my wife, she expressed no regret at the estrangement between her mother-in-law and herself. By common consent, we never spoke on that subject. We settled in the manufacturing town which I have already mentioned, and we kept a lodging-house. My kind master, at my request, granted me a lump sum in place of my annuity. This put us into a good house, decently furnished. For a while things went well enough. I may describe myself at this time of my life as a happy man.

My misfortunes began with a return of the complaint with which my mother had already suffered. The doctor confessed, when I asked him the question, that there was danger to be dreaded this time. Naturally, after hearing this, I was a good deal away at the cottage. Naturally also, I left the business of looking after the house, in my absence, to my wife. Little by little, I found her beginning to alter toward me. While my back was turned, she formed acquaintances with people of the doubtful and dissipated sort. One day, I observed something in her manner which forced the suspicion on me that she had been drinking. Before the week was out, my suspicion was a certainty. From keeping company with drunkards, she had grown to be a drunkard herself.

I did all a man could do to reclaim her. Quite useless! She had never really returned the love I felt for her: I had no influence; I could do nothing. My mother, hearing of this last worse trouble, resolved to try what her influence could do. Ill as she was, I found her one day dressed to go out.

"I am not long for this world, Francis," she said. "I shall not feel easy on my deathbed, unless I have done my best to the last to make you happy. I mean to put my own fears and my own feelings out of the question, and go with you to your wife, and try what I can do to reclaim her. Take me home with you, Francis. Let me do all I can to help my son, before it is too late."

How could I disobey her? We took the railway to the town: it was only half an hour's ride. By one o'clock in the afternoon we reached my house. It was our dinner hour, and Alicia was in the kitchen. I was able to take my mother quietly into the parlor and then to prepare my wife for the visit. She had drunk but little at that early hour; and, luckily, the devil in her was tamed for the time.

She followed me into the parlor, and the meeting passed off better than I had ventured to forecast; with this one drawback, that my mother, though she tried hard to control herself, shrank from looking my wife in the face when she spoke to her. It was a relief to me when Alicia began to prepare the table for dinner.

She laid the cloth, brought in the bread tray, and cut some slices for us from the loaf. Then she returned to the kitchen. At that moment, while I was still anxiously watching my mother, I was startled by seeing the same ghastly change pass over her face which had altered it in the morning when Alicia and she first met. Before I could say a word, she started up with a look of horror.

"Take me back! home, home again, Francis! Come with me, and never go back more!"

I was afraid to ask for an explanation; I could only sign her to be silent, and help her quickly to the door. As we passed the bread tray on the table, she stopped and pointed to it.

"Did you see what your wife cut your bread with?" she asked.

"No, mother; I was not noticing. What was it?"

"Look!"

I did look. A new clasp knife, with a buckhorn handle, lay with the loaf in the bread tray. I stretched out my hand to possess myself of it. At the same moment, there was a noise in the kitchen, and my mother caught me by the arm.

"The knife of the Dream! Francis, I'm faint with fear - take me away before she comes back!"

I couldn't speak to comfort or even to answer her. Superior as I was to superstition, the discovery of the knife staggered me. In silence, I helped my mother out of the house; and took her home.

I held out my hand to say good-by. She tried to stop me.

"Don't go back, Francis! don't go back!"

"I must get the knife, mother. I must go back by the next train." I held to that resolution. By the next train I went back.

XII

My wife had, of course, discovered our secret departure from the house. She had been drinking. She was in a fury of passion. The dinner in the kitchen was flung under the grate; the cloth was off the parlor table. Where was the knife?

I was foolish enough to ask for it. She refused to give it to me. In the course of the dispute between us which followed, I discovered that there was a horrible story attached to the knife. It had been used in a murder - years since - and had been so skillfully hidden that the authorities had been unable to produce it at the trial. By help of some of her disreputable friends, my wife had been able to purchase this relic of a bygone crime. Her perverted nature set some horrid unacknowledged value on the knife. Seeing there was no hope of getting it by fair means, I determined to search for it, later in the day, in secret. The search was unsuccessful. Night came on, and I left the house to walk about the streets. You will understand what a broken man I was by this time, when I tell you I was afraid to sleep in the same room with her!

Three weeks passed. Still she refused to give up the knife; and still that fear of sleeping in the same room with her possessed me. I walked about at night, or dozed in the parlor, or sat watching by my mother's bedside. Before the end of the first week in the new month, the worst misfortune of all befell me - my mother died. It wanted then but a short time to my birthday. She had longed to live till that day. I was present at her death. Her last words in this world were addressed to me. "Don't go back, my son - don't go back!"

I was obliged to go back, if it was only to watch my wife. In the last days of my mother's illness she had spitefully added a sting to my grief by declaring she would assert her right to attend the funeral. In spite of all that I could do or say, she held to her word. On the day appointed for the burial she forced herself, inflamed and shameless with drink, into my presence, and swore she would walk in the funeral procession to my mother's grave.

This last insult, after all I had gone through already, was more than I could endure. It maddened me. Try to make allowances for a man beside himself. I struck her.

The instant the blow was dealt, I repented it. She crouched down, silent, in a corner of the room, and eyed me steadily. It was a look that cooled my hot blood in an instant. There was no time now to think of making atonement. I could only risk the worst, and make sure of her till the funeral was over. I locked her into her bedroom.

When I came back, after laying my mother in the grave, I found her sitting by the bedside, very much altered in look and bearing, with a bundle on her lap. She faced me quietly; she spoke with a curious stillness in her voice; strangely and unnaturally composed in look and manner.

"No man has ever struck me yet," she said. "My husband shall have no second opportunity. Set the door open, and let me go."

She passed me, and left the room. I saw her walk away up the street. Was she gone for good?

All that night I watched and waited. No footstep came near the house. The next night, overcome with fatigue, I lay down on the bed in my clothes, with the door locked, the key on the table, and the candle burning. My slumber was not disturbed. The third night, the fourth, the fifth, the sixth, passed, and nothing happened. I lay down on the seventh night, still suspicious of something happening; still in my clothes; still with the door locked, the key on the table, and the candle burning.

My rest was disturbed. I awoke twice, without any sensation of uneasiness. The third time, that horrid shivering of the night at the lonely inn, that awful sinking pain at the heart, came back again, and roused me in an instant. My eyes turned to the left- hand side of the bed. And there stood, looking at me -

The Dream Woman again? No! My wife. The living woman, with the face of the Dream, in the attitude of the Dream, the fair arm up; the knife clasped in the delicate white hand.

I sprang upon her on the instant; but not quickly enough to stop her from hiding the knife. Without a word from me, without a cry from her, I pinioned her in a chair. With one hand I felt up her sleeve; and there, where the Dream Woman had hidden the knife, my wife had hidden it, the knife with the buckhorn handle, that looked like new.

What I felt when I made that discovery I could not realize at the time, and I can't describe now. I took one steady look at her with the knife in my hand. "You meant to kill me?" I said.

"Yes," she answered; "I meant to kill you." She crossed her arms over her bosom, and stared me coolly in the face. "I shall do it yet," she said. "With that knife."

I don't know what possessed me, I swear to you I am no coward; and yet I acted like a coward. The horrors got hold of me. I couldn't look at her, I couldn't speak to her. I left her (with the knife in my hand), and went out into the night.

There was a bleak wind abroad, and the smell of rain was in the air. The church clocks chimed the quarter as I walked beyond the last house in the town. I asked the first policeman I met what hour that was, of which the quarter past had just struck.

The man looked at his watch, and answered, "Two o'clock." Two in the morning. What day of the month was this day that had just begun? I reckoned it up from the date of my mother's funeral. The horrid parallel between the dream and the reality was complete - it was my birthday!

Had I escaped the mortal peril which the dream foretold? or had I only received a second warning? As that doubt crossed my mind I stopped on my way out of the town. The air had revived me, I felt in some degree like my own self again. After a little thinking, I began to see plainly the mistake I had made in leaving my wife free to go where she liked and to do as she pleased.

I turned instantly, and made my way back to the house. It was still dark. I had left the candle burning in the bedchamber. When I looked up to the window of the room now, there was no light in it. I advanced to the house door. On going away, I remembered to have closed it; on trying it now, I found it open.

I waited outside, never losing sight of the house till daylight. Then I ventured indoors, listened, and heard nothing, looked into the kitchen, scullery, parlor, and found nothing, went up at last into the bedroom. It was empty.

A picklock lay on the floor, which told me how she had gained entrance in the night. And that was the one trace I could find of the Dream Woman.

XIII

I waited in the house till the town was astir for the day, and then I went to consult a lawyer. In the confused state of my mind at the time, I had one clear notion of what I meant to do: I was determined to sell my house and leave the neighborhood. There were obstacles in the way which I had not counted on. I was told I had creditors to satisfy before I could leave, I, who had given my wife the money to pay my bills regularly every week! Inquiry showed that she had embezzled every farthing of the money I had intrusted to her. I had no choice but to pay over again.

Placed in this awkward position, my first duty was to set things right, with the help of my lawyer. During my forced sojourn in the town I did two foolish things. And, as a consequence that followed, I heard once more, and heard for the last time, of my wife.

In the first place, having got possession of the knife, I was rash enough to keep it in my pocket. In the second place, having something of importance to say to my lawyer, at a late hour of the evening, I went to his house after dark, alone and on foot. I got there safely enough. Returning, I was seized on from behind by two men, dragged down a passage and robbed, not only of the little money I had about me, but also of the knife. It was the lawyer's opinion (as it was mine) that the thieves were among the disreputable acquaintances formed by my wife, and that they, had attacked me at her instigation. To confirm this view I received a letter the next day, without date or address, written in Alicia's hand. The first line informed me that the knife was back again in her possession. The second line reminded me of the day when I struck her. The third line warned me that she would wash out the stain of that blow in my blood, and repeated the words, "I shall do it with the knife!"

These things happened a year ago. The law laid hands on the men who had robbed me; but from that time to this, the law has failed completely to find a trace of my wife.

My story is told. When I had paid the creditors and paid the legal expenses, I had barely five pounds left out of the sale of my house; and I had the world to begin over again. Some months since, drifting here and there, I found my way to Underbridge. The landlord of the inn had known something of my father's family in times past. He gave me (all he had to give) my food, and shelter in the yard. Except on market days, there is nothing to do. In the coming winter the inn is to be shut up, and I shall have to shift for myself. My old master would help me if I applied to him but I don't like to apply: he has done more for me already than I deserve. Besides, in another year who knows but my troubles may all be at an end? Next winter will bring me nigh to my next birthday, and my next birthday may be the day of my death. Yes! it's true I sat up all last night; and I heard two in the morning strike: and nothing happened. Still, allowing for that, the time to come is a time I don't trust. My wife has got the knife - my wife is looking for me. I am above superstition, mind! I don't say I believe in dreams; I only say, Alicia Warlock is looking for me. It is possible I may be wrong. It is possible I may be right. Who can tell?

THE THIRD NARRATIVE

THE STORY CONTINUED BY PERCY FAIRBANK

XIV

We took leave of Francis Raven at the door of Farleigh Hall, with the understanding that he might expect to hear from us again.

The same night Mrs. Fairbank and I had a discussion in the sanctuary of our own room. The topic was "The Hostler's Story"; and the question in dispute between us turned on the measure of charitable duty that we owed to the hostler himself.

The view I took of the man's narrative was of the purely matter-of- fact kind. Francis Raven had, in my opinion, brooded over the misty connection between his strange dream and his vile wife, until his mind was in a state of partial delusion on that subject. I was quite willing to help him with a trifle of money, and to recommend him to the kindness of my lawyer, if he was really in any danger and wanted advice. There my idea of my duty toward this afflicted person began and ended.

Confronted with this sensible view of the matter, Mrs. Fairbank's romantic temperament rushed, as usual, into extremes. "I should no more think of losing sight of Francis Raven when his next birthday comes round," says my wife, "than I should think of laying down a good story with the last chapters unread. I am positively determined, Percy, to take him back with us when we return to France, in the capacity of groom. What does one man more or less among the horses matter to people as rich as we are?" In this strain the partner of my joys and sorrows ran on, perfectly impenetrable to everything that I could say on the side of common sense. Need I tell my married brethren how it ended? Of course I allowed my wife to irritate me, and spoke to her sharply.

Of course my wife turned her face away indignantly on the conjugal pillow, and burst into tears. Of course upon that, "Mr." made his excuses, and "Mrs." had her own way.

Before the week was out we rode over to Underbridge, and duly offered to Francis Raven a place in our service as supernumerary groom.

At first the poor fellow seemed hardly able to realize his own extraordinary good fortune. Recovering himself, he expressed his gratitude modestly and becomingly. Mrs. Fairbank's ready sympathies overflowed, as usual, at her lips. She talked to him about our home in France, as if the worn, gray-headed hostler had been a child. "Such a dear old house, Francis; and such pretty gardens! Stables! Stables ten times as big as your stables here, quite a choice of rooms for you. You must learn the name of our house; Maison Rouge. Our nearest town is Metz. We are within a walk of the beautiful River Moselle. And when we want a change we have only to take the railway to the frontier, and find ourselves in Germany."

Listening, so far, with a very bewildered face, Francis started and changed color when my wife reached the end of her last sentence. "Germany?" he repeated.

"Yes. Does Germany remind you of anything?"

The hostler's eyes looked down sadly on the ground. "Germany reminds me of my wife," he replied.

"Indeed! How?"

"She once told me she had lived in Germany, long before I knew her, in the time when she was a young girl."

"Was she living with relations or friends?"

"She was living as governess in a foreign family."

"In what part of Germany?"

"I don't remember, ma'am. I doubt if she told me."

"Did she tell you the name of the family?"

"Yes, ma'am. It was a foreign name, and it has slipped my memory long since. The head of the family was a wine grower in a large way of business. I remember that."

"Did you hear what sort of wine he grew? There are wine growers in our neighborhood. Was it Moselle wine?"

"I couldn't say, ma'am, I doubt if I ever heard."

There the conversation dropped. We engaged to communicate with Francis Raven before we left England, and took our leave. I had made arrangements to pay our round of visits to English friends, and to return to Maison Rouge in the summer. On the eve of departure, certain difficulties in connection with the management of some landed property of mine in Ireland obliged us to alter our plans. Instead of getting back to our house in France in the Summer, we only returned a week or two before Christmas. Francis Raven accompanied us, and was duly established, in the nominal capacity of stable keeper, among the servants at Maison Rouge.

Before long, some of the objections to taking him into our employment, which I had foreseen and had vainly mentioned to my wife, forced themselves on our attention in no very agreeable form. Francis Raven failed (as I had feared he would) to get on smoothly with his fellow-servants. They were all French; and not one of them understood English. Francis, on his side, was equally ignorant of French. His reserved manners, his melancholy temperament, his solitary ways, all told against him. Our servants called him "the English Bear." He grew widely known in the neighborhood under his nickname. Quarrels took place, ending once or twice in blows. It became plain, even to Mrs. Fairbank herself, that some wise change must be made. While we were still considering what the change was to be, the unfortunate hostler was thrown on our hands for some time to come by an accident in the stables. Still pursued by his proverbial ill-luck, the poor wretch's leg was broken by a kick from a horse.

He was attended to by our own surgeon, in his comfortable bedroom at the stables. As the date of his birthday drew near, he was still confined to his bed.

Physically speaking, he was doing very well. Morally speaking, the surgeon was not satisfied. Francis Raven was suffering under some mysterious mental disturbance, which interfered seriously with his rest at night. Hearing this, I thought it my duty to tell the medical attendant what was preying on the patient's mind. As a practical man, he shared my opinion that the hostler was in a state of delusion on the subject of his Wife and his Dream. "Curable delusion, in my opinion," the surgeon added, "if the experiment could be fairly tried."

"How can it be tried?" I asked. Instead of replying, the surgeon put a question to me, on his side.

"Do you happen to know," he said, "that this year is Leap Year?"

"Mrs. Fairbank reminded me of it yesterday," I answered. "Otherwise I might NOT have known it."

"Do you think Francis Raven knows that this year is Leap Year?"

(I began to see dimly what my friend was driving at.)

"It depends," I answered, "on whether he has got an English almanac. Suppose he has NOT got the almanac, what then?"

"In that case," pursued the surgeon, "Francis Raven is innocent of all suspicion that there is a twenty-ninth day in February this year. As a necessary consequence what will he do? He will anticipate the appearance of the Woman with the Knife, at two in the morning of the twenty-ninth of February, instead of the first of March. Let him suffer all his superstitious terrors on the wrong day. Leave him, on the day that is really his birthday, to pass a perfectly quiet night, and to be as sound asleep as other people at two in the morning. And then, when he wakes comfortably in time for his breakfast, shame him out of his delusion by telling him the truth."

I agreed to try the experiment. Leaving the surgeon to caution Mrs. Fairbank on the subject of Leap Year, I went to the stables to see Mr. Raven.

XV

The poor fellow was full of forebodings of the fate in store for him on the ominous first of March. He eagerly entreated me to order one of the men servants to sit up with him on the birthday morning. In granting his request, I asked him to tell me on which day of the week his birthday fell. He reckoned the days on his fingers; and proved his innocence of all suspicion that it was Leap Year, by fixing on the twenty-ninth of February, in the full persuasion that it was the first of March. Pledged to try the surgeon's experiment, I left his error uncorrected, of course. In so doing, I took my first step blindfold toward the last act in the drama of the Hostler's Dream.

The next day brought with it a little domestic difficulty, which indirectly and strangely associated itself with the coming end.

My wife received a letter, inviting us to assist in celebrating the "Silver Wedding" of two worthy German neighbors of ours - Mr. and Mrs. Beldheimer. Mr. Beldheimer was a large wine grower on the banks of the Moselle. His house was situated on the frontier line of France and Germany; and the distance from our house was sufficiently considerable to make it necessary for us to sleep under our host's roof. Under these circumstances, if we accepted the invitation, a comparison of dates showed that we should be away from home on the morning of the first of March. Mrs. Fairbank, holding to her absurd resolution to see with her own eyes what might, or might not, happen to Francis Raven on his birthday, flatly declined to leave Maison Rouge. "It's easy to send an excuse," she said, in her off-hand manner.

I failed, for my part, to see any easy way out of the difficulty. The celebration of a "Silver Wedding" in Germany is the celebration of twenty-five years of happy married life; and the host's claim upon the consideration of his friends on such an occasion is something in the nature of a royal "command." After considerable discussion, finding my wife's obstinacy invincible, and feeling that the absence of both of us from the festival would certainly offend our friends, I left Mrs. Fairbank to make her excuses for herself, and directed her to accept the invitation so far as I was concerned. In so doing, I took my second step, blindfold, toward the last act in the drama of the Hostler's Dream.

A week elapsed; the last days of February were at hand. Another domestic difficulty happened; and, again, this event also proved to be strangely associated with the coming end.

My head groom at the stables was one Joseph Rigobert. He was an ill-conditioned fellow, inordinately vain of his personal appearance, and by no means scrupulous in his conduct with women. His one virtue consisted of his fondness for horses, and in the care he took of the animals under his charge. In a word, he was too good a groom to be easily replaced, or he would have quitted my service long since. On the occasion of which I am now writing, he was reported to me by my steward as growing idle and disorderly in his habits. The principal offense alleged against him was, that he had been seen that day in the city of Metz, in the company of a woman (supposed to be an Englishwoman), whom he was entertaining at a tavern, when he ought to have been on his way back to Maison Rouge. The man's defense was that "the lady" (as he called her) was an English stranger, unacquainted with the ways of the place, and that he had only shown her where she could obtain some refreshments at her own request. I administered the necessary reprimand, without troubling myself to inquire further into the matter. In failing to do this, I took my third step, blindfold, toward the last act in the drama of the Hostler's Dream.

On the evening of the twenty-eighth, I informed the servants at the stables that one of them must watch through the night by the Englishman's bedside. Joseph Rigobert immediately volunteered for the duty as a means, no doubt, of winning his way back to my favor. I accepted his proposal.

That day the surgeon dined with us. Toward midnight he and I left the smoking room, and repaired to Francis Raven's bedside. Rigobert was at his post, with no very agreeable expression on his face. The Frenchman and the Englishman had evidently not got on well together so far. Francis Raven lay helpless on his bed, waiting silently for two in the morning and the Dream Woman.

"I have come, Francis, to bid you good night," I said, cheerfully. "To-morrow morning I shall look in at breakfast time, before I leave home on a journey."

"Thank you for all your kindness, sir. You will not see me alive to-morrow morning. She will find me this time. Mark my words, she will find me this time."

"My good fellow! she couldn't find you in England. How in the world is she to find you in France?"

"It's borne in on my mind, sir, that she will find me here. At two in the morning on my birthday I shall see her again, and see her for the last time."

"Do you mean that she will kill you?"

"I mean that, sir, she will kill me - with the knife."

"And with Rigobert in the room to protect you?"

"I am a doomed man. Fifty Rigoberts couldn't protect me."

"And you wanted somebody to sit up with you?"

"Mere weakness, sir. I don't like to be left alone on my deathbed."

I looked at the surgeon. If he had encouraged me, I should certainly, out of sheer compassion, have confessed to Francis Raven the trick that we were playing him. The surgeon held to his experiment; the surgeon's face plainly said "No."

The next day (the twenty-ninth of February) was the day of the "Silver Wedding." The first thing in the morning, I went to Francis Raven's room. Rigobert met me at the door.

"How has he passed the night?" I asked.

"Saying his prayers, and looking for ghosts," Rigobert answered. "A lunatic asylum is the only proper place for him."

I approached the bedside. "Well, Francis, here you are, safe and sound, in spite of what you said to me last night."

His eyes rested on mine with a vacant, wondering look.

"I don't understand it," he said.

"Did you see anything of your wife when the clock struck two?"

"No, sir."

"Did anything happen?"

"Nothing happened, sir."

"Doesn't THIS satisfy you that you were wrong?"

His eyes still kept their vacant, wondering look. He only repeated the words he had spoken already: "I don't understand it."

I made a last attempt to cheer him. "Come, come, Francis! keep a good heart. You will be out of bed in a fortnight."

He shook his head on the pillow. "There's something wrong," he said. "I don't expect you to believe me, sir. I only say there's something wrong and time will show it."

I left the room. Half an hour later I started for Mr. Beldheimer's house; leaving the arrangements for the morning of the first of March in the hands of the doctor and my wife.

XVI

The one thing which principally struck me when I joined the guests at the "Silver Wedding" is also the one thing which it is necessary to mention here. On this joyful occasion a noticeable lady present was out of spirits. That lady was no other than the heroine of the festival, the mistress of the house!

In the course of the evening I spoke to Mr. Beldheimer's eldest son on the subject of his mother. As an old friend of the family, I had a claim on his confidence which the young man willingly recognized.

"We have had a very disagreeable matter to deal with," he said; "and my mother has not recovered the painful impression left on her mind. Many years since, when my sisters were children, we had an English governess in the house. She left us, as we then understood, to be married. We heard no more of her until a week or ten days since, when my mother received a letter, in which our ex- governess described herself as being in a condition of great poverty and distress. After much hesitation she had ventured, at the suggestion of a lady who had been kind to her, to write to her former employers, and to appeal to their remembrance of old times. You know my mother she is not only the most kind-headed, but the most innocent of women, it is impossible to persuade her of the wickedness that there is in the world. She replied by return of post, inviting the governess to come here and see her, and inclosing the money for her traveling expenses. When my father came home, and heard what had been done, he wrote at once to his agent in London to make inquiries, inclosing the address on the governess' letter. Before he could receive the agent's reply the governess arrived. She produced the worst possible impression on his mind. The agent's letter, arriving a few days later, confirmed his suspicions. Since we had lost sight of her, the woman had led a most disreputable life. My father spoke to her privately: he offered, on condition of her leaving the house, a sum of money to take her back to England. If she refused, the alternative would be an appeal to the authorities and a public scandal. She accepted the money, and left the house. On her way back to England she appears to have stopped at Metz. You will understand what sort of woman she is when I tell you that she was seen the other day in a tavern with your handsome groom, Joseph Rigobert."

While my informant was relating these circumstances, my memory was at work. I recalled what Francis Raven had vaguely told us of his wife's experience in former days as governess in a German family. A suspicion of the truth suddenly flashed across my mind. "What was the woman's name?" I asked.

Mr. Beldheimer's son answered: "Alicia Warlock."

I had but one idea when I heard that reply, to get back to my house without a moment's needless delay. It was then ten o'clock at night, the last train to Metz had left long since. I arranged with my young friend, after duly informing him of the circumstances, that I should go by the first train in the morning, instead of staying to breakfast with the other guests who slept in the house.

At intervals during the night I wondered uneasily how things were going on at Maison Rouge. Again and again the same question occurred to me, on my journey home in the early morning, the morning of the first of March. As the event proved, but one person in my house knew what really happened at the stables on Francis Raven's birthday. Let Joseph Rigobert take my place as narrator, and tell the story of the end to You, as he told it, in times past, to his lawyer and to Me.

FOURTH (AND LAST) NARRATIVE

STATEMENT OF JOSEPH RIGOBERT: ADDRESSED TO THE ADVOCATE WHO DEFENDED HIM AT HIS TRIAL

RESPECTED SIR, On the twenty-seventh of February I was sent, on business connected with the stables at Maison Rouge, to the city of Metz. On the public promenade I met a magnificent woman. Complexion, blond. Nationality, English. We mutually admired each other; we fell into conversation. (She spoke French perfectly with the English accent.) I offered refreshment; my proposal was accepted. We had a long and interesting interview, we discovered that we were made for each other. So far, Who is to blame?

Is it my fault that I am a handsome man, universally agreeable as such to the fair sex? Is it a criminal offense to be accessible to the amiable weakness of love? I ask again, Who is to blame? Clearly, nature. Not the beautiful lady, not my humble self.

To resume. The most hard-hearted person living will understand that two beings made for each other could not possibly part without an appointment to meet again.

I made arrangements for the accommodation of the lady in the village near Maison Rouge. She consented to honor me with her company at supper, in my apartment at the stables, on the night of the twenty-ninth. The time fixed on was the time when the other servants were accustomed to retire, eleven o'clock.

Among the grooms attached to the stables was an Englishman, laid up with a broken leg. His name was Francis. His manners were repulsive; he was ignorant of the French language. In the kitchen he went by the nickname of the "English Bear." Strange to say, he was a great favorite with my master and my mistress. They even humored certain superstitious terrors to which this repulsive person was subject, terrors into the nature of which I, as an advanced freethinker, never thought it worth my while to inquire.

On the evening of the twenty-eighth the Englishman, being a prey to the terrors which I have mentioned, requested that one of his fellow-servants might sit up with him for that night only. The wish that he expressed was backed by Mr. Fairbank's authority. Having already incurred my master's displeasure, in what way, a proper sense of my own dignity forbids me to relate, I volunteered to watch by the bedside of the English Bear. My object was to satisfy Mr. Fairbank that I bore no malice, on my side, after what had occurred between us. The wretched Englishman passed a night of delirium. Not understanding his barbarous language, I could only gather from his gesture that he was in deadly fear of some fancied apparition at his bedside. From time to time, when this madman disturbed my slumbers, I quieted him by swearing at him. This is the shortest and best way of dealing with persons in his condition.

On the morning of the twenty-ninth, Mr. Fairbank left us on a journey. Later in the day, to my unspeakable disgust, I found that I had not done with the Englishman yet. In Mr. Fairbank's absence, Mrs. Fairbank took an incomprehensible interest in the question of my delirious fellow-servant's repose at night. Again, one or the other of us was to watch at his bedside, and report it, if anything happened. Expecting my fair friend to supper, it was necessary to make sure that the other servants at the stables would be safe in their beds that night. Accordingly, I volunteered once more to be the man who kept watch. Mrs. Fairbank complimented me on my humanity. I possess great command over my feelings. I accepted the compliment without a blush.

Twice, after nightfall, my mistress and the doctor (the last staying in the house in Mr. Fairbank's absence) came to make inquiries. Once BEFORE the arrival of my fair friend and once AFTER. On the second occasion (my apartment being next door to the Englishman's) I was obliged to hide my charming guest in the harness room. She consented, with angelic resignation, to immolate her dignity to the servile necessities of my position. A more amiable woman (so far) I never met with!

After the second visit I was left free. It was then close on midnight. Up to that time there was nothing in the behavior of the mad Englishman to reward Mrs. Fairbank and the doctor for presenting themselves at his bedside. He lay half awake, half asleep, with an odd wondering kind of look in his face. My mistress at parting warned me to be particularly watchful of him toward two in the morning. The doctor (in case anything happened) left me a large hand bell to ring, which could easily be heard at the house.

Restored to the society of my fair friend, I spread the supper table. A pate, a sausage, and a few bottles of generous Moselle wine, composed our simple meal. When persons adore each other, the intoxicating illusion of Love transforms the simplest meal into a banquet. With immeasurable capacities for enjoyment, we sat down to table. At the very moment when I placed my fascinating companion in a chair, the infamous Englishman in the next room took that occasion, of all others, to become restless and noisy once more. He struck with his stick on the floor; he cried out, in a delirious access of terror, "Rigobert! Rigobert!"

The sound of that lamentable voice, suddenly assailing our ears, terrified my fair friend. She lost all her charming color in an instant. "Good heavens!" she exclaimed. "Who is that in the next room?"

"A mad Englishman."

"An Englishman?"

"Compose yourself, my angel. I will quiet him." The lamentable voice called out on me again, "Rigobert! Rigobert!"

My fair friend caught me by the arm. "Who is he?" she cried. "What is his name?"

Something in her face struck me as she put that question. A spasm of jealousy shook me to the soul. "You know him?" I said.

"His name!" she vehemently repeated; "his name!"

"Francis," I answered.

"Francis WHAT?"

I shrugged my shoulders. I could neither remember nor pronounce the barbarous English surname. I could only tell her it began with an "R."

She dropped back into the chair. Was she going to faint? No: she recovered, and more than recovered, her lost color. Her eyes flashed superbly. What did it mean? Profoundly as I understand women in general, I was puzzled by THIS woman!

"You know him?" I repeated.

She laughed at me. "What nonsense! How should I know him? Go and quiet the wretch."

My looking-glass was near. One glance at it satisfied me that no woman in her senses could prefer the Englishman to Me. I recovered my self-respect. I hastened to the Englishman's bedside.

The moment I appeared he pointed eagerly toward my room. He overwhelmed me with a torrent of words in his own language. I made out, from his gestures and his looks, that he had, in some incomprehensible manner, discovered the presence of my guest; and, stranger still, that he was scared by the idea of a person in my room. I endeavored to compose him on the system which I have already mentioned that is to say, I swore at him in MY language. The result not proving satisfactory, I own I shook my fist in his face, and left the bedchamber.

Returning to my fair friend, I found her walking backward and forward in a state of excitement wonderful to behold. She had not waited for me to fill her glass, she had begun the generous Moselle in my absence. I prevailed on her with difficulty to place herself at the table. Nothing would induce her to eat. "My appetite is gone," she said. "Give me wine."

The generous Moselle deserves its name, delicate on the palate, with prodigious "body." The strength of this fine wine produced no stupefying effect on my remarkable guest. It appeared to strengthen and exhilarate her, nothing more. She always spoke in the same low tone, and always, turn the conversation as I might, brought it back with the same dexterity to the subject of the Englishman in the next room. In any other woman this persistency would have offended me. My lovely guest was irresistible; I answered her questions with the docility of a child. She possessed all the amusing eccentricity of her nation. When I told her of the accident which confined the Englishman to his bed, she sprang to her feet. An extraordinary smile irradiated her countenance. She said, "Show me the horse who broke the Englishman's leg! I must see that horse!" I took her to the stables. She kissed the horse - on my word of honor, she kissed the horse! That struck me. I said. "You DO know the man; and he has wronged you in some way." No! she would not admit it, even then. "I kiss all beautiful animals," she said. "Haven't I kissed YOU?" With that charming explanation of her conduct, she ran back up the stairs. I only remained behind to lock the stable door again. When I rejoined her, I made a startling discovery. I caught her coming out of the Englishman's room.

"I was just going downstairs again to call you," she said. "The man in there is getting noisy once more."

The mad Englishman's voice assailed our ears once again. "Rigobert! Rigobert!"

He was a frightful object to look at when I saw him this time. His eyes were staring wildly; the perspiration was pouring over his face. In a panic of terror he clasped his hands; he pointed up to heaven. By every sign and gesture that a man can make, he entreated me not to leave him again. I really could not help smiling. The idea of my staying with HIM, and leaving my fair friend by herself in the next room!

I turned to the door. When the mad wretch saw me leaving him he burst out into a screech of despair so shrill that I feared it might awaken the sleeping servants.

My presence of mind in emergencies is proverbial among those who know me. I tore open the cupboard in which he kept his linen, seized a handful of his handkerchief's, gagged him with one of them, and secured his hands with the others. There was now no danger of his alarming the servants. After tying the last knot, I looked up.

The door between the Englishman's room and mine was open. My fair friend was standing on the threshold, watching HIM as he lay helpless on the bed; watching ME as I tied the last knot.

"What are you doing there?" I asked. "Why did you open the door?"

She stepped up to me, and whispered her answer in my ear, with her eyes all the time upon the man on the bed:

"I heard him scream."

"Well?"

"I thought you had killed him."

I drew back from her in horror. The suspicion of me which her words implied was sufficiently detestable in itself. But her manner when she uttered the words was more revolting still. It so powerfully affected me that I started back from that beautiful creature as I might have recoiled from a reptile crawling over my flesh.

Before I had recovered myself sufficiently to reply, my nerves were assailed by another shock. I suddenly heard my mistress's voice calling to me from the stable yard.

There was no time to think - there was only time to act. The one thing needed was to keep Mrs. Fairbank from ascending the stairs, and discovering, not my lady guest only, but the Englishman also, gagged and bound on his bed. I instantly hurried to the yard. As I ran down the stairs I heard the stable clock strike the quarter to two in the morning.

My mistress was eager and agitated. The doctor (in attendance on her) was smiling to himself, like a man amused at his own thoughts.

"Is Francis awake or asleep?" Mrs. Fairbank inquired.

"He has been a little restless, madam. But he is now quiet again. If he is not disturbed" (I added those words to prevent her from ascending the stairs), "he will soon fall off into a quiet sleep."

"Has nothing happened since I was here last?"

"Nothing, madam."

The doctor lifted his eyebrows with a comical look of distress. "Alas, alas, Mrs. Fairbank!" he said. "Nothing has happened! The days of romance are over!"

"It is not two o'clock yet," my mistress answered, a little irritably.

The smell of the stables was strong on the morning air. She put her handkerchief to her nose and led the way out of the yard by the north entrance, the entrance communicating with the gardens and the house. I was ordered to follow her, along with the doctor. Once out of the smell of the stables she began to question me again. She was unwilling to believe that nothing had occurred in her absence. I invented the best answers I could think of on the spur of the moment; and the doctor stood by laughing. So the minutes passed till the clock struck two. Upon that, Mrs. Fairbank announced her intention of personally visiting the Englishman in his room. To my great relief, the doctor interfered to stop her from doing this.

"You have heard that Francis is just falling asleep," he said. "If you enter his room you may disturb him. It is essential to the success of my experiment that he should have a good night's rest, and that he should own it himself, before I tell him the truth. I must request, madam, that you will not disturb the man. Rigobert will ring the alarm bell if anything happens."

My mistress was unwilling to yield. For the next five minutes, at least, there was a warm discussion between the two. In the end Mrs. Fairbank was obliged to give way for the time. "In half an hour," she said, "Francis will either be sound asleep, or awake again. In half an hour I shall come back." She took the doctor's arm. They returned together to the house.

Left by myself, with half an hour before me, I resolved to take the Englishwoman back to the village, then, returning to the stables, to remove the gag and the bindings from Francis, and to let him screech to his heart's content. What would his alarming the whole establishment matter to ME after I had got rid of the compromising presence of my guest?

Returning to the yard I heard a sound like the creaking of an open door on its hinges. The gate of the north entrance I had just closed with my own hand. I went round to the west entrance, at the back of the stables. It opened on a field crossed by two footpaths in Mr. Fairbank's grounds. The nearest footpath led to the village. The other led to the highroad and the river.

Arriving at the west entrance I found the door open, swinging to and fro slowly in the fresh morning breeze. I had myself locked and bolted that door after admitting my fair friend at eleven o'clock. A vague dread of something wrong stole its way into my mind. I hurried back to the stables.

I looked into my own room. It was empty. I went to the harness room. Not a sign of the woman was there. I returned to my room, and approached the door of the Englishman's bedchamber. Was it possible that she had remained there during my absence? An unaccountable reluctance to open the door made me hesitate, with my hand on the lock. I listened. There was not a sound inside. I called softly. There was no answer. I drew back a step, still hesitating. I noticed something dark moving slowly in the crevice between the bottom of the door and the boarded floor. Snatching up the candle from the table, I held it low, and looked. The dark, slowly moving object was a stream of blood!

That horrid sight roused me. I opened the door. The Englishman lay on his bed, alone in the room. He was stabbed in two places, in the throat and in the heart. The weapon was left in the second wound. It was a knife of English manufacture, with a handle of buckhorn as good as new.

I instantly gave the alarm. Witnesses can speak to what followed. It is monstrous to suppose that I am guilty of the murder. I admit that I am capable of committing follies: but I shrink from the bare idea of a crime. Besides, I had no motive for killing the man. The woman murdered him in my absence. The woman escaped by the west entrance while I was talking to my mistress. I have no more to say. I swear to you what I have here written is a true statement of all that happened on the morning of the first of March.

Accept, sir, the assurance of my sentiments of profound gratitude and respect.

JOSEPH RIGOBERT.

LAST LINES ADDED BY PERCY FAIRBANK

Tried for the murder of Francis Raven, Joseph Rigobert was found Not Guilty; the papers of the assassinated man presented ample evidence of the deadly animosity felt toward him by his wife.

The investigations pursued on the morning when the crime was committed showed that the murderess, after leaving the stable, had taken the footpath which led to the river. The river was dragged, without result. It remains doubtful to this day whether she died by drowning or not. The one thing certain is that Alicia Warlock was never seen again.

So beginning in mystery, ending in mystery the Dream Woman passes from your view. Ghost; demon; or living human creature say for yourselves which she is. Or, knowing what unfathomed wonders are around you, what unfathomed wonders are IN you, let the wise words of the greatest of all poets be explanation enough:

"We are such stuff
As dreams are made of,
and our little life
Is rounded with a sleep."

The Traveler's Story Of A Terribly Strange Bed

Shortly after my education at college was finished, I happened to be staying at Paris with an English friend. We were both young men then, and lived, I am afraid, rather a wild life, in the delightful city of our sojourn. One night we were idling about the neighbourhood of the Palais Royal, doubtful to what amusement we should next betake ourselves. My friend proposed a visit to Frascati's; but his suggestion was not to my taste. I knew Frascati's, as the French saying is, by heart; had lost and won plenty of five-franc pieces there, merely for amusement's sake, until it was amusement no longer, and was thoroughly tired, in fact, of all the ghastly respectabilities of such a social anomaly as a respectable gambling-house. 'For Heaven's sake,' said I to my friend, 'let us go somewhere where we can see a little genuine, blackguard, poverty-stricken gaming with no false gingerbread glitter thrown over it all. Let us get away from fashionable Frascati's, to a house where they don't mind letting in a man with a ragged coat, or a man with no coat, ragged or otherwise.' 'Very well,' said my friend, 'we needn't go out of the Palais Royal to find the sort of company you want. Here's the place just before us; as blackguard a place, by all report, as you could possibly wish to see.' In another minute we arrived at the door and entered the house.

When we got upstairs, and had left our hats and sticks with the doorkeeper, we were admitted into the chief gambling-room. We did not find many people assembled there. But, few as the men were who looked up at us on our entrance, they were all types, lamentably true types, of their respective classes.

We had come to see blackguards; but these men were something worse. There is a comic side, more or less appreciable, in all blackguardism--here there was nothing but tragedy; mute, weird tragedy. The quiet in the room was horrible. The thin, haggard, long-haired young man, whose sunken eyes fiercely watched the turning up of the cards, never spoke; the flabby, fat-faced, pimply player, who pricked his piece of pasteboard perseveringly, to register how often black won, and how often red--never spoke; the dirty, wrinkled old man, with the vulture eyes and the darned great-coat, who had lost his last sou, and still looked on desperately, after he could play no longer - never spoke. Even the voice of the croupier sounded as if it were strangely dulled and thickened in the atmosphere of the room. I had entered the place to laugh, but the spectacle before me was something to weep over. I soon found it necessary to take refuge in excitement from the depression of spirits which was fast stealing on me. Unfortunately I sought the nearest excitement, by going to the table and beginning to play. Still more unfortunately, as the event will show, I won, won prodigiously; won incredibly; won at such a rate that the regular players at the table crowded round me; and staring at my stakes with hungry, superstitious eyes, whispered to one another that the English stranger was going to break the bank.

The game was Rouge et Noir. I had played at it in every city in Europe, without, however, the care or the wish to study the Theory of Chances, that philosopher's stone of all gamblers! And a gambler, in the strict sense of the word, I had never been. I was heart-whole from the corroding passion for play. My gaming was a mere idle amusement. I never resorted to it by necessity, because I never knew what it was to want money. I never practised it so incessantly as to lose more than I could afford, or to gain more than I could coolly pocket without being thrown off my balance by my good luck. In short, I had hitherto frequented gambling-tables, just as I frequented ball-rooms and opera-houses, because they amused me, and because I had nothing better to do with my leisure hours.

But on this occasion it was very different, now, for the first time in my life, I felt what the passion for play really was. My success first bewildered, and then, in the most literal meaning of the word, intoxicated me. Incredible as it may appear, it is nevertheless true, that I only lost when I attempted to estimate chances, and played according to previous calculation. If I left everything to luck, and staked without any care or consideration, I was sure to win, to win in the face of every recognized probability in favour of the bank. At first some of the men present ventured their money safely enough on my colour; but I speedily increased my stakes to sums which they dared not risk. One after another they left off playing, and breathlessly looked on at my game.

Still, time after time, I staked higher and higher, and still won. The excitement in the room rose to fever pitch. The silence was interrupted by a deep-muttered chorus of oaths and exclamations in different languages, every time the gold was shovelled across to my side of the table, even the imperturbable croupier dashed his rake on the floor in a (French) fury of astonishment at my success. But one man present preserved his self-possession, and that man was my friend. He came to my side, and whispering in English, begged me to leave the place, satisfied with what I had already gained. I must do him the justice to say that he repeated his warnings and entreaties several times, and only left me and went away after I had rejected his advice (I was to all intents and purposes gambling drunk) in terms which rendered it impossible for him to address me again that night.

Shortly after he had gone, a hoarse voice behind me cried: 'Permit me, my dear sir, permit me to restore to their proper place two napoleons which you have dropped. Wonderful luck, sir! I pledge you my word of honour, as an old soldier, in the course of my long experience in this sort of thing, I never saw such luck as yours - never! Go on, sir - Sacre mille bombes! Go on boldly, and break the bank!'

I turned round and saw, nodding and smiling at me with inveterate civility, a tall man, dressed in a frogged and braided surtout.

If I had been in my senses, I should have considered him, personally, as being rather a suspicious specimen of an old soldier. He had goggling bloodshot eyes, mangy moustaches, and a broken nose. His voice betrayed a barrack-room intonation of the worst order, and he had the dirtiest pair of hands I ever saw, even in France. These little personal peculiarities exercised, however, no repelling influence on me. In the mad excitement, the reckless triumph of that moment, I was ready to 'fraternize' with anybody who encouraged me in my game. I accepted the old soldier's offered pinch of snuff; clapped him on the back, and swore he was the honestest fellow in the world, the most glorious relic of the Grand Army that I had ever met with. 'Go on!' cried my military friend, snapping his fingers in ecstasy - 'Go on, and win! Break the bank - Mille tonnerres! my gallant English comrade, break the bank!'

And I did go on, went on at such a rate, that in another quarter of an hour the croupier called out, 'Gentlemen, the bank has discontinued for tonight.' All the notes, and all the gold in that 'bank', now lay in a heap under my hands; the whole floating capital of the gambling-house was waiting to pour into my pockets!

'Tie up the money in your pocket-handkerchief, my worthy sir,' said the old soldier, as I wildly plunged my hands into my heap of gold. 'Tie it up, as we used to tie up a bit of dinner in the Grand Army; your winnings are too heavy for any breeches-pockets that ever were sewed. There! that's it, shovel them in, notes and all! Credie! what luck! Stop! another napoleon on the floor! Ah! sacre petit polisson de Napoleon! have I found thee at last? Now then, sir, two tight double knots each way with your honourable permission, and the money's safe. Feel it! feel it, fortunate sir! hard and round as a cannon-ball - Ah, bah! if they had only fired such cannon-balls at us at Austerlitz - nom d'une pipe! if they only had! And now, as an ancient grenadier, as an ex-brave of the French army, what remains for me to do? I ask what? Simply this: to entreat my valued English friend to drink a bottle of champagne with me, and toast the goddess Fortune in foaming goblets before we part!'

Excellent ex-brave! Convivial ancient grenadier! Champagne by all means! An English cheer for an old soldier! Hurrah! hurrah! Another English cheer for the goddess Fortune! Hurrah! hurrah! hurrah!

'Bravo! the Englishman; the amiable, gracious Englishman, in whose veins circulates the vivacious blood of France! Another glass? Ah, bah! the bottle is empty! Never mind! Vive le vin! I, the old soldier, order another bottle, and half a pound of bonbons with it!'

'No, no, ex-brave; never, ancient grenadier! Your bottle last time; my bottle this. Behold it! Toast away! The French Army! the great Napoleon! the present company! the croupier! the honest croupier's wife and daughters - if he has any! the Ladies generally! everybody in the world!'

By the time the second bottle of champagne was emptied, I felt as if I had been drinking liquid fire, my brain seemed all aflame. No excess in wine had ever had this effect on me before in my life. Was it the result of a stimulant acting upon my system when I was in a highly excited state? Was my stomach in a particularly disordered condition? Or was the champagne amazingly strong?

'Ex-brave of the French Army!' cried I, in a mad state of exhilaration, 'I am on fire! how are you? You have set me on fire. Do you hear, my hero of Austerlitz? Let us have a third bottle of champagne to put the flame out!'

The old soldier wagged his head, rolled his goggle-eyes, until I expected to see them slip out of their sockets; placed his dirty forefinger by the side of his broken nose; solemnly ejaculated 'Coffee!' and immediately ran off into an inner room.

The word pronounced by the eccentric veteran seemed to have a magical effect on the rest of the company present. With one accord they all rose to depart. Probably they had expected to profit by my intoxication; but finding that my new friend was benevolently bent on preventing me from getting dead drunk, had now abandoned all hope of thriving pleasantly on my winnings. Whatever their motive might be, at any rate they went away in a body. When the old soldier returned, and sat down again opposite to me at the table, we had the room to ourselves. I could see the croupier, in a sort of vestibule which opened out of it, eating his supper in solitude. The silence was now deeper than ever.

A sudden change, too, had come over the 'ex-brave'. He assumed a portentously solemn look; and when he spoke to me again, his speech was ornamented by no oaths, enforced by no finger-snapping, enlivened by no apostrophes or exclamations.

'Listen, my dear sir,' said he, in mysteriously confidential tones 'listen to an old soldier's advice. I have been to the mistress of the house (a very charming woman, with a genius for cookery!) to impress on her the necessity of making us some particularly strong and good coffee. You must drink this coffee in order to get rid of your little amiable exaltation of spirits before you think of going home, you must, my good and gracious friend! With all that money to take home to-night, it is a sacred duty to yourself to have your wits about you. You are known to be a winner to an enormous extent by several gentlemen present to-night, who, in a certain point of view, are very worthy and excellent fellows; but they are mortal men, my dear sir, and they have their amiable weaknesses. Need I say more? Ah, no, no! you understand me! Now, this is what you must do, send for a cabriolet when you feel quite well again draw up all the windows when you get into it and tell the driver to take you home only through the large and well-lighted thoroughfares. Do this; and you and your money will be safe. Do this; and to-morrow you will thank an old soldier for giving you a word of honest advice.'

Just as the ex-brave ended his oration in very lachrymose tones, the coffee came in, ready poured out in two cups. My attentive friend handed me one of the cups with a bow. I was parched with thirst, and drank it off at a draught. Almost instantly afterwards, I was seized with a fit of giddiness, and felt more completely intoxicated than ever. The room whirled round and round furiously; the old soldier seemed to be regularly bobbing up and down before me like the piston of a steam-engine. I was half deafened by a violent singing in my ears; a feeling of utter bewilderment, helplessness, idiocy, overcame me. I rose from my chair, holding on by the table to keep my balance; and stammered out that I felt dreadfully unwell--so unwell that I did not know how I was to get home.

'My dear friend,' answered the old soldier--and even his voice seemed to be bobbing up and down as he spoke 'my dear friend, it would be madness to go home in your state; you would be sure to lose your money; you might be robbed and murdered with the greatest ease. I am going to sleep here; do you sleep here, too, they make up capital beds in this house, take one; sleep off the effects of the wine, and go home safely with your winnings to-morrow--to-morrow, in broad daylight.'

I had but two ideas left: one, that I must never let go hold of my handkerchief full of money; the other, that I must lie down somewhere immediately, and fall off into a comfortable sleep. So I agreed to the proposal about the bed, and took the offered arm of the old soldier, carrying my money with my disengaged hand. Preceded by the croupier, we passed along some passages and up a flight of stairs into the bedroom which I was to occupy. The ex-brave shook me warmly by the hand, proposed that we should breakfast together, and then, followed by the croupier, left me for the night.

I ran to the wash-hand stand; drank some of the water in my jug; poured the rest out, and plunged my face into it; then sat down in a chair and tried to compose myself. I soon felt better. The change for my lungs, from the fetid atmosphere of the gambling-room to the cool air of the apartment I now occupied, the almost equally refreshing change for my eyes, from the glaring gaslights of the 'salon' to the dim, quiet flicker of one bedroom-candle, aided wonderfully the restorative effects of cold water. The giddiness left me, and I began to feel a little like a reasonable being again. My first thought was of the risk of sleeping all night in a gambling-house; my second, of the still greater risk of trying to get out after the house was closed, and of going home alone at night through the streets of Paris with a large sum of money about me. I had slept in worse places than this on my travels; so I determined to lock, bolt, and barricade my door, and take my chance till the next morning.

Accordingly, I secured myself against all intrusion; looked under the bed, and into the cupboard; tried the fastening of the window; and then, satisfied that I had taken every proper precaution, pulled off my upper clothing, put my light, which was a dim one, on the hearth among a feathery litter of wood-ashes, and got into bed, with the handkerchief full of money under my pillow.

I soon felt not only that I could not go to sleep, but that I could not even close my eyes. I was wide awake, and in a high fever. Every nerve in my body trembled, every one of my senses seemed to be preternaturally sharpened. I tossed and rolled, and tried every kind of position, and perseveringly sought out the cold corners of the bed, and all to no purpose. Now I thrust my arms over the clothes; now I poked them under the clothes; now I violently shot my legs straight out down to the bottom of the bed; now I convulsively coiled them up as near my chin as they would go; now I shook out my crumpled pillow, changed it to the cool side, patted it flat, and lay down quietly on my back; now I fiercely doubled it in two, set it up on end, thrust it against the board of the bed, and tried a sitting posture. Every effort was in vain; I groaned with vexation as I felt that I was in for a sleepless night.

What could I do? I had no book to read. And yet, unless I found out some method of diverting my mind, I felt certain that I was in the condition to imagine all sorts of horrors; to rack my brain with forebodings of every possible and impossible danger; in short, to pass the night in suffering all conceivable varieties of nervous terror.

I raised myself on my elbow, and looked about the room, which was brightened by a lovely moonlight pouring straight through the window, to see if it contained any pictures or ornaments that I could at all clearly distinguish. While my eyes wandered from wall to wall, a remembrance of Le Maistre's delightful little book, Voyage autour de ma Chambre, occurred to me. I resolved to imitate the French author, and find occupation and amusement enough to relieve the tedium of my wakefulness, by making a mental inventory of every article of furniture I could see, and by following up to their sources the multitude of associations which even a chair, a table, or a wash-hand stand may be made to call forth.

In the nervous unsettled state of my mind at that moment, I found it much easier to make my inventory than to make my reflections, and thereupon soon gave up all hope of thinking in Le Maistre's fanciful track--or, indeed, of thinking at all. I looked about the room at the different articles of furniture, and did nothing more.

There was, first, the bed I was lying in; a four-post bed, of all things in the world to meet with in Paris, yes, a thorough clumsy British four-poster, with the regular top lined with chintz, the regular fringed valance all round, the regular stifling, unwholesome curtains, which I remembered having mechanically drawn back against the posts without particularly noticing the bed when I first got into the room. Then there was the marble-topped wash-hand stand, from which the water I had spilled, in my hurry to pour it out, was still dripping, slowly and more slowly, on to the brick floor. Then two small chairs, with my coat, waistcoat, and trousers flung on them. Then a large elbow-chair covered with dirty-white dimity, with my cravat and shirt collar thrown over the back. Then a chest of drawers with two of the brass handles off, and a tawdry, broken china inkstand placed on it by way of ornament for the top. Then the dressing-table, adorned by a very small looking-glass, and a very large pincushion. Then the window, an unusually large window. Then a dark old picture, which the feeble candle dimly showed me. It was a picture of a fellow in a high Spanish hat, crowned with a plume of towering feathers. A swarthy, sinister ruffian, looking upward, shading his eyes with his hand, and looking intently upward, it might be at some tall gallows at which he was going to be hanged. At any rate, he had the appearance of thoroughly deserving it.

This picture put a kind of constraint upon me to look upward too, at the top of the bed. It was a gloomy and not an interesting object, and I looked back at the picture. I counted the feathers in the man's hat, they stood out in relief, three white, two green. I observed the crown of his hat, which was of conical shape, according to the fashion supposed to have been favoured by Guido Fawkes. I wondered what he was looking up at. It couldn't be at the stars; such a desperado was neither astrologer nor astronomer. It must be at the high gallows, and he was going to be hanged presently. Would the executioner come into possession of his conical crowned hat and plume of feathers? I counted the feathers again – three white, two green.

While I still lingered over this very improving and intellectual employment, my thoughts insensibly began to wander. The moonlight shining into the room reminded me of a certain moonlight night in England the night after a picnic party in a Welsh valley. Every incident of the drive homeward, through lovely scenery, which the moonlight made lovelier than ever, came back to my remembrance, though I had never given the picnic a thought for years; though, if I had tried to recollect it, I could certainly have recalled little or nothing of that scene long past. Of all the wonderful faculties that help to tell us we are immortal, which speaks the sublime truth more eloquently than memory? Here was I, in a strange house of the most suspicious character, in a situation of uncertainty, and even of peril, which might seem to make the cool exercise of my recollection almost out of the question; nevertheless, remembering, quite involuntarily, places, people, conversations, minute circumstances of every kind, which I had thought forgotten for ever; which I could not possibly have recalled at will, even under the most favourable auspices. And what cause had produced in a moment the whole of this strange, complicated, mysterious effect? Nothing but some rays of moonlight shining in at my bedroom window.

I was still thinking of the picnic, of our merriment on the drive home, of the sentimental young lady who would quote 'Childe Harold' because it was moonlight. I was absorbed by these past scenes and past amusements, when, in an instant, the thread on which my memories hung snapped asunder; my attention immediately came back to present things more vividly than ever, and I found myself, I neither knew why nor wherefore, looking hard at the picture again.

Looking for what?

Good God! the man had pulled his hat down on his brows! No! the hat itself was gone! Where was the conical crown? Where the feathers, three white, two green? Not there! In place of the hat and feathers, what dusky object was it that now hid his forehead, his eyes, his shading hand?

Was the bed moving?

I turned on my back and looked up. Was I mad? drunk? dreaming? giddy again? or was the top of the bed really moving down, sinking slowly, regularly, silently, horribly, right down throughout the whole of its length and breadth, right down upon me, as I lay underneath?

My blood seemed to stand still. A deadly paralysing coldness stole all over me as I turned my head round on the pillow and determined to test whether the bed-top was really moving or not, by keeping my eye on the man in the picture.

The next look in that direction was enough. The dull, black, frowzy outline of the valance above me was within an inch of being parallel with his waist. I still looked breathlessly. And steadily and slowly, very slowly, I saw the figure, and the line of frame below the figure, vanish, as the valance moved down before it.

I am, constitutionally, anything but timid. I have been on more than one occasion in peril of my life, and have not lost my self-possession for an instant; but when the conviction first settled on my mind that the bed-top was really moving, was steadily and continuously sinking down upon me, I looked up shuddering, helpless, panic-stricken, beneath the hideous machinery for murder, which was advancing closer and closer to suffocate me where I lay.

I looked up, motionless, speechless, breathless. The candle, fully spent, went out; but the moonlight still brightened the room. Down and down, without pausing and without sounding, came the bed-top, and still my panic-terror seemed to bind me faster and faster to the mattress on which I lay, down and down it sank, till the dusty odour from the lining of the canopy came stealing into my nostrils.

At that final moment the instinct of self-preservation startled me out of my trance, and I moved at last. There was just room for me to roll myself sidewise off the bed. As I dropped noiselessly to the floor, the edge of the murderous canopy touched me on the shoulder.

Without stopping to draw my breath, without wiping the cold sweat from my face, I rose instantly on my knees to watch the bed-top. I was literally spellbound by it. If I had heard footsteps behind me, I could not have turned round; if a means of escape had been miraculously provided for me, I could not have moved to take advantage of it. The whole life in me was, at that moment, concentrated in my eyes.

It descended the whole canopy, with the fringe round it, came down, down, close down; so close that there was not room now to squeeze my finger between the bed-top and the bed. I felt at the sides, and discovered that what had appeared to me from beneath to be the ordinary light canopy of a four-post bed was in reality a thick, broad mattress, the substance of which was concealed by the valance and its fringe. I looked up and saw the four posts rising hideously bare. In the middle of the bed-top was a huge wooden screw that had evidently worked it down through a hole in the ceiling, just as ordinary presses are worked down on the substance selected for compression. The frightful apparatus moved without making the faintest noise. There had been no creaking as it came down; there was now not the faintest sound from the room above. Amid a dead and awful silence I beheld before me in the nineteenth century, and in the civilized capital of France such a machine for secret murder by suffocation as might have existed in the worst days of the Inquisition, in the lonely inns among the Hartz Mountains, in the mysterious tribunals of Westphalia! Still, as I looked on it, I could not move, I could hardly breathe, but I began to recover the power of thinking, and in a moment I discovered the murderous conspiracy framed against me in all its horror.

My cup of coffee had been drugged, and drugged too strongly. I had been saved from being smothered by having taken an overdose of some narcotic. How I had chafed and fretted at the fever-fit which had preserved my life by keeping me awake! How recklessly I had confided myself to the two wretches who had led me into this room, determined, for the sake of my winnings, to kill me in my sleep by the surest and most horrible contrivance for secretly accomplishing my destruction! How many men, winners like me, had slept, as I had proposed to sleep, in that bed, and had never been seen or heard of more! I shuddered at the bare idea of it.

But, ere long, all thought was again suspended by the sight of the murderous canopy moving once more. After it had remained on the bed, as nearly as I could guess, about ten minutes, it began to move up again. The villains who worked it from above evidently believed that their purpose was now accomplished. Slowly and silently, as it had descended, that horrible bed-top rose towards its former place. When it reached the upper extremities of the four posts, it reached the ceiling, too. Neither hole nor screw could be seen; the bed became in appearance an ordinary bed again, the canopy an ordinary canopy, even to the most suspicious eyes.

Now, for the first time, I was able to move, to rise from my knees, to dress myself in my upper clothing and to consider of how I should escape. If I betrayed by the smallest noise that the attempt to suffocate me had failed, I was certain to be murdered. Had I made any noise already? I listened intently, looking towards the door.

No! no footsteps in the passage outside, no sound of a tread, light or heavy, in the room above, absolute silence everywhere. Besides locking and bolting my door, I had moved an old wooden chest against it, which I had found under the bed. To remove this chest (my blood ran cold as I thought of what its contents might be!) without making some disturbance was impossible; and, moreover, to think of escaping through the house, now barred up for the night, was sheer insanity. Only one chance was left me - the window. I stole to it on tiptoe.

My bedroom was on the first floor, above an entresol, and looked into a back street. I raised my hand to open the window, knowing that on that action hung, by the merest hair-breadth, my chance of safety. They keep vigilant watch in a House of Murder. If any part of the frame cracked, if the hinge creaked, I was a lost man! It must have occupied me at least five minutes, reckoning by time, five hours, reckoning by suspense, to open that window. I succeeded in doing it silently, in doing it with all the dexterity of a house-breaker, and then looked down into the street. To leap the distance beneath me would be almost certain destruction! Next, I looked round at the sides of the house. Down the left side ran a thick water-pipe--it passed close by the outer edge of the window. The moment I saw the pipe I knew I was saved. My breath came and went freely for the first time since I had seen the canopy of the bed moving down upon me!

To some men the means of escape which I had discovered might have seemed difficult and dangerous enough, to me the prospect of slipping down the pipe into the street did not suggest even a thought of peril. I had always been accustomed, by the practice of gymnastics, to keep up my schoolboy powers as a daring and expert climber; and knew that my head, hands, and feet would serve me faithfully in any hazards of ascent or descent. I had already got one leg over the window-sill, when I remembered the handkerchief filled with money under my pillow. I could well have afforded to leave it behind me, but I was revengefully determined that the miscreants of the gambling-house should miss their plunder as well as their victim. So I went back to the bed and tied the heavy handkerchief at my back by my cravat.

Just as I had made it tight and fixed it in a comfortable place, I thought I heard a sound of breathing outside the door. The chill feeling of horror ran through me again as I listened.

No! dead silence still in the passage, I had only heard the night air blowing softly into the room. The next moment I was on the window-sill and the next I had a firm grip on the water-pipe with my hands and knees.

I slid down into the street easily and quietly, as I thought I should, and immediately set off at the top of my speed to a branch "Prefecture" of Police, which I knew was situated in the immediate neighbourhood. A "Sub-prefect", and several picked men among his subordinates, happened to be up, maturing, I believe, some scheme for discovering the perpetrator of a mysterious murder which all Paris was talking of just then. When I began my story, in a breathless hurry and in very bad French, I could see that the Sub-prefect suspected me of being a drunken Englishman who had robbed somebody; but he soon altered his opinion as I went on, and before I had anything like concluded, he shoved all the papers before him into a drawer, put on his hat, supplied me with another (for I was bareheaded), ordered a file of soldiers, desired his expert followers to get ready all sorts of tools for breaking open doors and ripping up brick flooring, and took my arm, in the most friendly and familiar manner possible, to lead me with him out of the house. I will venture to say that when the Sub-prefect was a little boy, and was taken for the first time to the play, he was not half as much pleased as he was now at the job in prospect for him at the gambling-house!

Away we went through the streets, the Sub-prefect cross-examining and congratulating me in the same breath as we marched at the head of our formidable posse comitatus. Sentinels were placed at the back and front of the house the moment we got to it; a tremendous battery of knocks was directed against the door; a light appeared at a window; I was told to conceal myself behind the police, then came more knocks and a cry of 'Open in the name of the law!' At that terrible summons bolts and locks gave way before an invisible hand, and the moment after the Sub-prefect was in the passage, confronting a waiter half-dressed and ghastly pale. This was the short dialogue which immediately took place:

'We want to see the Englishman who is sleeping in this house?'

'He went away hours ago.'

'He did no such thing. His friend went away; he remained. Show us to his bedroom!'

'I swear to you, Monsieur le Sous-prefect, he is not here! He -'

'I swear to you, Monsieur le Garcon, he is. He slept here, he didn't find your bed comfortable he came to us to complain of it, here he is among my men, and here am I ready to look for a flea or two in his bedstead. Renaudin!' calling to one of the subordinates, and pointing to the waiter 'collar that man and tie his hands behind him. Now, then, gentlemen, let us walk upstairs!'

Every man and woman in the house was secured, the 'Old Soldier' the first. Then I identified the bed in which I had slept, and then we went into the room above.

No object that was at all extraordinary appeared in any part of it. The Sub-prefect looked round the place, commanded everybody to be silent, stamped twice on the floor, called for a candle, looked attentively at the spot he had stamped on, and ordered the flooring there to be carefully taken up. This was done in no time. Lights were produced, and we saw a deep raftered cavity between the floor of this room and the ceiling of the room beneath. Through this cavity there ran perpendicularly a sort of case of iron thickly greased; and inside the case appeared the screw, which communicated with the bed-top below. Extra lengths of screw, freshly oiled; levers covered with felt; all the complete upper works of a heavy press, constructed with infernal ingenuity so as to join the fixtures below, and when taken to pieces again, to go into the smallest possible compass were next discovered and pulled out on the floor. After some little difficulty the Sub-prefect succeeded in putting the machinery together, and, leaving his men to work it, descended with me to the bedroom. The smothering canopy was then lowered, but not so noiselessly as I had seen it lowered. When I mentioned this to the Sub-prefect, his answer, simple as it was, had a terrible significance. 'My men,' said he, 'are working down the bed-top for the first time, the men whose money you won were in better practice.'

We left the house in the sole possession of two police agents, every one of the inmates being removed to prison on the spot. The Sub-prefect, after taking down my process verbal in his office, returned with me to my hotel to get my passport. 'Do you think,' I asked, as I gave it to him, 'that any men have really been smothered in that bed, as they tried to smother me?'

'I have seen dozens of drowned men laid out at the Morgue,' answered the Sub-prefect, 'in whose pocketbooks were found letters stating that they had committed suicide in the Seine, because they had lost everything at the gaming table. Do I know how many of those men entered the same gambling-house that you entered? won as you won? took that bed as you took it? slept in it? were smothered in it? and were privately thrown into the river, with a letter of explanation written by the murderers and placed in their pocket-books? No man can say how many or how few have suffered the fate from which you have escaped. The people of the gambling-house kept their bedstead machinery a secret from us, even from the police! The dead kept the rest of the secret for them. Good night, or rather good morning, Monsieur Faulkner! Be at my office again at nine o'clock--in the meantime, au revoir!'

The rest of my story is soon told. I was examined and re-examined; the gambling-house was strictly searched all through from top to bottom; the prisoners were separately interrogated; and two of the less guilty among them made a confession. I discovered that the Old Soldier was the master of the gambling-house, justice discovered that he had been drummed out of the army as a vagabond years ago; that he had been guilty of all sorts of villainies since; that he was in possession of stolen property, which the owners identified; and that he, the croupier, another accomplice, and the woman who had made my cup of coffee, were all in the secret of the bedstead. There appeared some reason to doubt whether the inferior persons attached to the house knew anything of the suffocating machinery; and they received the benefit of that doubt, by being treated simply as thieves and vagabonds. As for the Old Soldier and his two head myrmidons, they went to the galleys; the woman who had drugged my coffee was imprisoned for I forget how many years; the regular attendants at the gambling-house were considered 'suspicious' and placed under 'surveillance'; and I became, for one whole week (which is a long time) the head 'lion' in Parisian society. My adventure was dramatized by three illustrious playmakers, but never saw theatrical daylight; for the censorship forbade the introduction on the stage of a correct copy of the gambling-house bedstead.

One good result was produced by my adventure, which any censorship must have approved: it cured me of ever again trying Rouge et Noir as an amusement. The sight of a green cloth, with packs of cards and heaps of money on it, will henceforth be for ever associated in my mind with the sight of a bed canopy descending to suffocate me in the silence and darkness of the night.

The Dead Alive

CHAPTER I. THE SICK MAN.

"HEART all right," said the doctor. "Lungs all right. No organic disease that I can discover. Philip Lefrank, don't alarm yourself. You are not going to die yet. The disease you are suffering from is overwork. The remedy in your case is rest."

So the doctor spoke, in my chambers in the Temple (London); having been sent for to see me about half an hour after I had alarmed my clerk by fainting at my desk. I have no wish to intrude myself needlessly on the reader's attention; but it may be necessary to add, in the way of explanation, that I am a "junior" barrister in good practice. I come from the channel Island of Jersey. The French spelling of my name (Lefranc) was Anglicized generations since, in the days when the letter "k" was still used in England at the end of words which now terminate in "c." We hold our heads high, nevertheless, as a Jersey family. It is to this day a trial to my father to hear his son described as a member of the English bar.

"Rest!" I repeated, when my medical adviser had done. "My good friend, are you aware that it is term-time? The courts are sitting. Look at the briefs waiting for me on that table! Rest means ruin in my case."

"And work," added the doctor, quietly, "means death."

I started. He was not trying to frighten me: he was plainly in earnest.

"It is merely a question of time," he went on. "You have a fine constitution; you are a young man; but you cannot deliberately overwork your brain, and derange your nervous system, much longer. Go away at once. If you are a good sailor, take a sea-voyage. The ocean air is the best of all air to build you up again. No: I don't want to write a prescription. I decline to physic you. I have no more to say."

With these words my medical friend left the room. I was obstinate: I went into court the same day.

The senior counsel in the case on which I was engaged applied to me for some information which it was my duty to give him. To my horror and amazement, I was perfectly unable to collect my ideas; facts and dates all mingled together confusedly in my mind. I was led out of court thoroughly terrified about myself. The next day my briefs went back to the attorneys; and I followed my doctor's advice by taking my passage for America in the first steamer that sailed for New York.

I had chosen the voyage to America in preference to any other trip by sea, with a special object in view. A relative of my mother's had emigrated to the United States many years since, and had thriven there as a farmer. He had given me a general invitation to visit him if I ever crossed the Atlantic. The long period of inaction, under the name of rest, to which the doctor's decision had condemned me, could hardly be more pleasantly occupied, as I thought, than by paying a visit to my relation, and seeing what I could of America in that way. After a brief sojourn at New York, I started by railway for the residence of my host, Mr. Isaac Meadowcroft, of Morwick Farm.

There are some of the grandest natural prospects on the face of creation in America. There is also to be found in certain States of the Union, by way of wholesome contrast, scenery as flat, as monotonous, and as uninteresting to the traveler, as any that the earth can show. The part of the country in which M. Meadowcroft's farm was situated fell within this latter category. I looked round me when I stepped out of the railway-carriage on the platform at Morwick Station; and I said to myself, "If to be cured means, in my case, to be dull, I have accurately picked out the very place for the purpose."

I look back at those words by the light of later events; and I pronounce them, as you will soon pronounce them, to be the words of an essentially rash man, whose hasty judgment never stopped to consider what surprises time and chance together might have in store for him.

Mr. Meadowcroft's eldest son, Ambrose, was waiting at the station to drive me to the farm.

There was no forewarning, in the appearance of Ambrose Meadowcroft, of the strange and terrible events that were to follow my arrival at Morwick. A healthy, handsome young fellow, one of thousands of other healthy, handsome young fellows, said, "How d'ye do, Mr. Lefrank? Glad to see you, sir. Jump into the buggy; the man will look after your portmanteau." With equally conventional politeness I answered, "Thank you. How are you all at home?" So we started on the way to the farm.

Our conversation on the drive began with the subjects of agriculture and breeding. I displayed my total ignorance of crops and cattle before we had traveled ten yards on our journey. Ambrose Meadowcroft cast about for another topic, and failed to find it. Upon this I cast about on my side, and asked, at a venture, if I had chosen a convenient time for my visit The young farmer's stolid brown face instantly brightened. I had evidently hit, hap-hazard, on an interesting subject.

"You couldn't have chosen a better time," he said. "Our house has never been so cheerful as it is now."

"Have you any visitors staying with you?"

"It's not exactly a visitor. It's a new member of the family who has come to live with us."

"A new member of the family! May I ask who it is?"

Ambrose Meadowcroft considered before he replied; touched his horse with the whip; looked at me with a certain sheepish hesitation; and suddenly burst out with the truth, in the plainest possible words:

"It's just the nicest girl, sir, you ever saw in your life."

"Ay, ay! A friend of your sister's, I suppose?"

"A friend? Bless your heart! it's our little American cousin, Naomi Colebrook."

I vaguely remembered that a younger sister of Mr. Meadowcroft's had married an American merchant in the remote past, and had died many years since, leaving an only child. I was now further informed that the father also was dead. In his last moments he had committed his helpless daughter to the compassionate care of his wife's relations at Morwick.

"He was always a speculating man," Ambrose went on. "Tried one thing after another, and failed in all. Died, sir, leaving barely enough to bury him. My father was a little doubtful, before she came here, how his American niece would turn out. We are English, you know; and, though we do live in the United States, we stick fast to our English ways and habits. We don't much like American women in general, I can tell you; but when Naomi made her appearance she conquered us all. Such a girl! Took her place as one of the family directly. Learned to make herself useful in the dairy in a week's time. I tell you this--she hasn't been with us quite two months yet, and we wonder already how we ever got on without her!"

Once started on the subject of Naomi Colebrook, Ambrose held to that one topic and talked on it without intermission. It required no great gift of penetration to discover the impression which the American cousin had produced in this case. The young fellow's enthusiasm communicated itself, in a certain tepid degree, to me. I really felt a mild flutter of anticipation at the prospect of seeing Naomi, when we drew up, toward the close of evening, at the gates of Morwick Farm.

CHAPTER II. THE NEW FACES.

Immediatley on my arrival, I was presented to Mr. Meadowcroft, the father.

The old man had become a confirmed invalid, confined by chronic rheumatism to his chair. He received me kindly, and a little wearily as well. His only unmarried daughter (he had long since been left a widower) was in the room, in attendance on her father. She was a melancholy, middle-aged woman, without visible attractions of any sort, one of those persons who appear to accept the obligation of living under protest, as a burden which they would never have consented to bear if they had only been consulted first. We three had a dreary little interview in a parlor of bare walls; and then I was permitted to go upstairs, and unpack my portmanteau in my own room.

"Supper will be at nine o'clock, sir," said Miss Meadowcroft.

She pronounced those words as if "supper" was a form of domestic offense, habitually committed by the men, and endured by the women. I followed the groom up to my room, not over-well pleased with my first experience of the farm.

No Naomi and no romance, thus far!

My room was clean oppressively clean. I quite longed to see a little dust somewhere. My library was limited to the Bible and the Prayer-book. My view from the window showed me a dead flat in a partial state of cultivation, fading sadly from view in the waning light. Above the head of my spruce white bed hung a scroll, bearing a damnatory quotation from Scripture in emblazoned letters of red and black. The dismal presence of Miss Meadowcroft had passed over my bedroom, and had blighted it. My spirits sank as I looked round me. Supper-time was still an event in the future. I lighted the candles and took from my portmanteau what I firmly believe to have been the first French novel ever produced at Morwick Farm. It was one of the masterly and charming stories of Dumas the elder. In five minutes I was in a new world, and my melancholy room was full of the liveliest French company. The sound of an imperative and uncompromising bell recalled me in due time to the regions of reality. I looked at my watch. Nine o'clock.

Ambrose met me at the bottom of the stairs, and showed me the way to the supper-room.

Mr. Meadowcroft's invalid chair had been wheeled to the head of the table. On his right-hand side sat his sad and silent daughter. She signed to me, with a ghostly solemnity, to take the vacant place on the left of her father. Silas Meadowcroft came in at the same moment, and was presented to me by his brother. There was a strong family likeness between them, Ambrose being the taller and the handsomer man of the two. But there was no marked character in either face. I set them down as men with undeveloped qualities, waiting (the good and evil qualities alike) for time and circumstances to bring them to their full growth.

The door opened again while I was still studying the two brothers, without, I honestly confess, being very favorably impressed by either of them. A new member of the family circle, who instantly attracted my attention, entered the room.

He was short, spare, and wiry; singularly pale for a person whose life was passed in the country. The face was in other respects, besides this, a striking face to see. As to the lower part, it was covered with a thick black beard and mustache, at a time when shaving was the rule, and beards the rare exception, in America. As to the upper part of the face, it was irradiated by a pair of wild, glittering brown eyes, the expression of which suggested to me that there was something not quite right with the man's mental balance. A perfectly sane person in all his sayings and doings, so far as I could see, there was still something in those wild brown eyes which suggested to me that, under exceptionally trying circumstances, he might surprise his oldest friends by acting in some exceptionally violent or foolish way. "A little cracked" that in the popular phrase was my impression of the stranger who now made his appearance in the supper-room.

Mr. Meadowcroft the elder, having not spoken one word thus far, himself introduced the newcomer to me, with a side-glance at his sons, which had something like defiance in it, a glance which, as I was sorry to notice, was returned with the defiance on their side by the two young men.

"Philip Lefrank, this is my overlooker, Mr. Jago," said the old man, formally presenting us. "John Jago, this is my young relative by marriage, Mr. Lefrank. He is not well; he has come over the ocean for rest, and change of scene. Mr. Jago is an American, Philip. I hope you have no prejudice against Americans. Make acquaintance with Mr. Jago. Sit together." He cast another dark look at his sons; and the sons again returned it. They pointedly drew back from John Jago as he approached the empty chair next to me and moved round to the opposite side of the table. It was plain that the man with the beard stood high in the father's favor, and that he was cordially disliked for that or for some other reason by the sons.

The door opened once more. A young lady quietly joined the party at the supper-table.

Was the young lady Naomi Colebrook? I looked at Ambrose, and saw the answer in his face. Naomi Colebrook at last!

A pretty girl, and, so far as I could judge by appearances, a good girl too. Describing her generally, I may say that she had a small head, well carried, and well set on her shoulders; bright gray eyes, that looked at you honestly, and meant what they looked; a trim, slight little figure,too slight for our English notions of beauty; a strong American accent; and (a rare thing in America) a pleasantly toned voice, which made the accent agreeable to English ears. Our first impressions of people are, in nine cases out of ten, the right impressions. I liked Naomi Colebrook at first sight; liked her pleasant smile; liked her hearty shake of the hand when we were presented to each other. "If I get on well with nobody else in this house," I thought to myself, "I shall certainly get on well with you."

For once in a way, I proved a true prophet. In the atmosphere of smoldering enmities at Morwick Farm, the pretty American girl and I remained firm and true friends from first to last. Ambrose made room for Naomi to sit between his brother and himself. She changed color for a moment, and looked at him, with a pretty, reluctant tenderness, as she took her chair. I strongly suspected the young farmer of squeezing her hand privately, under cover of the tablecloth.

The supper was not a merry one. The only cheerful conversation was the conversation across the table between Naomi and me.

For some incomprehensible reason, John Jago seemed to be ill at ease in the presence of his young countrywoman. He looked up at Naomi doubtingly from his plate, and looked down again slowly with a frown. When I addressed him, he answered constrainedly. Even when he spoke to Mr. Meadowcroft, he was still on his guard--on his guard against the two young men, as I fancied by the direction which his eyes took on these occasions. When we began our meal, I had noticed for the first time that Silas Meadowcroft's left hand was strapped up with surgical plaster; and I now further observed that John Jago's wandering brown eyes, furtively looking at everybody round the table in turn, looked with a curious, cynical scrutiny at the young man's injured hand.

By way of making my first evening at the farm all the more embarrassing to me as a stranger, I discovered before long that the father and sons were talking indirectly at each other, through Mr. Jago and through me. When old Mr. Meadowcroft spoke disparagingly to his overlooker of some past mistake made in the cultivation of the arable land of the farm, old Mr. Meadowcroft's eyes pointed the application of his hostile criticism straight in the direction of his two sons When the two sons seized a stray remark of mine about animals in general, and applied it satirically to the mismanagement of sheep and oxen in particular, they looked at John Jago, while they talked to me. On occasions of this sort and they happened frequently, Naomi struck in resolutely at the right moment, and turned the talk to some harmless topic. Every time she took a prominent part in this way in keeping the peace, melancholy Miss Meadowcroft looked slowly round at her in stern and silent disparagement of her interference. A more dreary and more disunited family party I never sat at the table with. Envy, hatred, malice and uncharitableness are never so essentially detestable to my mind as when they are animated by a sense of propriety, and work under the surface. But for my interest in Naomi, and my other interest in the little love-looks which I now and then surprised passing between her and Ambrose, I should never have sat through that supper. I should certainly have taken refuge in my French novel and my own room.

At last the unendurably long meal, served with ostentatious profusion, was at an end. Miss Meadowcroft rose with her ghostly solemnity, and granted me my dismissal in these words:

"We are early people at the farm, Mr. Lefrank. I wish you good-night."

She laid her bony hands on the back of Mr. Meadowcroft's invalid-chair, cut him short in his farewell salutation to me, and wheeled him out to his bed as if she were wheeling him out to his grave.

"Do you go to your room immediately, sir? If not, may I offer you a cigar, provided the young gentlemen will permit it?"

So, picking his words with painful deliberation, and pointing his reference to "the young gentlemen" with one sardonic side-look at them, Mr. John Jago performed the duties of hospitality on his side. I excused myself from accepting the cigar. With studied politeness, the man of the glittering brown eyes wished me a goodnight's rest, and left the room.

Ambrose and Silas both approached me hospitably, with their open cigar-cases in their hands.

"You were quite right to say 'No,'" Ambrose began. "Never smoke with John Jago. His cigars will poison you."

"And never believe a word John Jago says to you," added Silas. "He is the greatest liar in America, let the other be whom he may."

Naomi shook her forefinger reproachfully at them, as if the two sturdy young farmers had been two children.

"What will Mr. Lefrank think," she said, "if you talk in that way of a person whom your father respects and trusts? Go and smoke. I am ashamed of both of you."

Silas slunk away without a word of protest. Ambrose stood his ground, evidently bent on making his peace with Naomi before he left her.

Seeing that I was in the way, I walked aside toward a glass door at the lower end of the room. The door opened on the trim little farm-garden, bathed at that moment in lovely moonlight. I stepped out to enjoy the scene, and found my way to a seat under an elm-tree. The grand repose of nature had never looked so unutterably solemn and beautiful as it now appeared, after what I had seen and heard inside the house. I understood, or thought I understood, the sad despair of humanity which led men into monasteries in the old times. The misanthropical side of my nature (where is the sick man who is not conscious of that side of him?) was fast getting the upper hand of me when I felt a light touch laid on my shoulder, and found myself reconciled to my species once more by Naomi Colebrook.

CHAPTER III. THE MOONLIGHT MEETING.

"I want to speak to you," Naomi began "You don't think ill of me for following you out here? We are not accustomed to stand much on ceremony in America."

"You are quite right in America. Pray sit down."

She seated herself by my side, looking at me frankly and fearlessly by the light of the moon.

"You are related to the family here," she resumed, "and I am related too. I guess I may say to you what I couldn't say to a stranger. I am right glad you have come here, Mr. Lefrank; and for a reason, sir, which you don't suspect."

"Thank you for the compliment you pay me, Miss Colebrook, whatever the reason may be."

She took no notice of my reply; she steadily pursued her own train of thought.

"I guess you may do some good, sir, in this wretched house," the girl went on, with her eyes still earnestly fixed on my face. "There is no love, no trust, no peace, at Morwick Farm. They want somebody here, except Ambrose. Don't think ill of Ambrose; he is only thoughtless. I say, the rest of them want somebody here to make them ashamed of their hard hearts, and their horrid, false, envious ways. You are a gentleman; you know more than they know; they can't help themselves; they must look up to you. Try, Mr. Lefrank, when you have the opportunity, pray try, sir, to make peace among them. You heard what went on at supper-time; and you were disgusted with it. Oh yes, you were! I saw you frown to yourself; and I know what that means in you Englishmen."

There was no choice but to speak one's mind plainly to Naomi. I acknowledged the impression which had been produced on me at supper-time just as plainly as I have acknowledged it in these pages. Naomi nodded her head in undisguised approval of my candor.

"That will do, that's speaking out," she said. "But, oh my! you put it a deal too mildly, sir, when you say the men don't seem to be on friendly terms together here. They hate each other. That's the word, Mr. Lefrank, hate; bitter, bitter, bitter hate!" She clinched her little fists; she shook them vehemently, by way of adding emphasis to her last words; and then she suddenly remembered Ambrose. "Except Ambrose," she added, opening her hand again, and laying it very earnestly on my arm. "Don't go and misjudge Ambrose, sir. There is no harm in poor Ambrose."

The girl's innocent frankness was really irresistible.

"Should I be altogether wrong," I asked, "if I guessed that you were a little partial to Ambrose?"

An Englishwoman would have felt, or would at least have assumed, some little hesitation at replying to my question. Naomi did not hesitate for an instant.

"You are quite right, sir," she said with the most perfect composure. "If things go well, I mean to marry Ambrose."

"If things go well," I repeated. "What does that mean? Money?"

She shook her head.

"It means a fear that I have in my own mind," she answered "a fear, Mr. Lefrank, of matters taking a bad turn among the men here, the wicked, hard-hearted, unfeeling men. I don't mean Ambrose, sir; I mean his brother Silas, and John Jago. Did you notice Silas's hand? John Jago did that, sir, with a knife."

"By accident?" I asked.

"On purpose," she answered. "In return for a blow."

This plain revelation of the state of things at Morwick Farm rather staggered me - blows and knives under the rich and respectable roof-tree of old Mr. Meadowcroft--blows and knives, not among the laborers, but among the masters! My first impression was like your first impression, no doubt. I could hardly believe it.

"Are you sure of what you say?" I inquired.

"I have it from Ambrose. Ambrose would never deceive me. Ambrose knows all about it."

My curiosity was powerfully excited. To what sort of household had I rashly voyaged across the ocean in search of rest and quiet?

"May I know all about it too?" I said.

"Well, I will try and tell you what Ambrose told me. But you must promise me one thing first, sir. Promise you won't go away and leave us when you know the whole truth. Shake hands on it, Mr. Lefrank; come, shake hands on it."

There was no resisting her fearless frankness. I shook hands on it. Naomi entered on her narrative the moment I had given her my pledge, without wasting a word by way of preface.

"When you are shown over the farm here," she began, "you will see that it is really two farms in one. On this side of it, as we look from under this tree, they raise crops: on the other side, on much the larger half of the land, mind they raise cattle. When Mr. Meadowcroft got too old and too sick to look after his farm himself, the boys (I mean Ambrose and Silas) divided the work between them. Ambrose looked after the crops, and Silas after the cattle. Things didn't go well, somehow, under their management. I can't tell you why. I am only sure Ambrose was not in fault. The old man got more and more dissatisfied, especially about his beasts. His pride is in his beasts. Without saying a word to the boys, he looked about privately (I think he was wrong in that, sir; don't you?) he looked about privately for help; and, in an evil hour, he heard of John Jago. Do you like John Jago, Mr. Lefrank?"

"So far, no. I don't like him."

"Just my sentiments, sir. But I don't know: it's likely we may be wrong. There's nothing against John Jago, except that he is so odd in his ways. They do say he wears all that nasty hair on his face (I hate hair on a man's face) on account of a vow he made when he lost his wife. Don't you think, Mr. Lefrank, a man must be a little mad who shows his grief at losing his wife by vowing that he will never shave himself again? Well, that's what they do say John Jago vowed. Perhaps it's a lie. People are such liars here! Anyway, it's truth (the boys themselves confess that), when John came to the farm, he came with a first-rate character. The old father here isn't easy to please; and he pleased the old father. Yes, that's so. Mr. Meadowcroft don't like my countrymen in general. He's like his sons - English, bitter English, to the marrow of his bones. Somehow, in spite of that, John Jago got round him; maybe because John does certainly know his business. Oh yes! Cattle and crops, John knows his business. Since he's been overlooker, things have prospered as they didn't prosper in the time of the boys. Ambrose owned as much to me himself. Still, sir, it's hard to be set aside for a stranger; isn't it? John gives the orders now. The boys do their work; but they have no voice in it when John and the old man put their heads together over the business of the farm. I have been long in telling you of it, sir, but now you know how the envy and the hatred grew among the men before my time. Since I have been here, things seem to get worse and worse. There's hardly a day goes by that hard words don't pass between the boys and John, or the boys and their father. The old man has an aggravating way, Mr. Lefrank--a nasty way, as we do call it--of taking John Jago's part. Do speak to him about it when you get the chance. The main blame of the quarrel between Silas and John the other day lies at his door, as I think. I don't want to excuse Silas, either. It was brutal of him, though he is Ambrose's brother to strike John, who is the smaller and weaker man of the two. But it was worse than brutal in John, sir, to out with his knife and try to stab Silas. Oh, he did it! If Silas had not caught the knife in his hand (his hand's awfully cut, I can tell you; I dressed it myself), it might have ended, for anything I know, in murder -"

She stopped as the word passed her lips, looked back over her shoulder, and started violently.

I looked where my companion was looking. The dark figure of a man was standing, watching us, in the shadow of the elm-tree. I rose directly to approach him. Naomi recovered her self-possession, and checked me before I could interfere.

"Who are you?" she asked, turning sharply toward the stranger. "What do you want there?"

The man stepped out from the shadow into the moonlight, and stood revealed to us as John Jago.

"I hope I am not intruding?" he said, looking hard at me.

"What do you want?" Naomi repeated.

"I don't wish to disturb you, or to disturb this gentleman," he proceeded. "When you are quite at leisure, Miss Naomi, you would be doing me a favor if you would permit me to say a few words to you in private."

He spoke with the most scrupulous politeness; trying, and trying vainly, to conceal some strong agitation which was in possession of him. His wild brown eyes, wilder than ever in the moonlight, rested entreatingly, with a strange underlying expression of despair, on Naomi's face. His hands, clasped lightly in front of him, trembled incessantly. Little as I liked the man, he did really impress me as a pitiable object at that moment.

"Do you mean that you want to speak to me to-night?" Naomi asked, in undisguised surprise.

"Yes, miss, if you please, at your leisure and at Mr. Lefrank's."

Naomi hesitated.

"Won't it keep till to-morrow?" she said.

"I shall be away on farm business to-morrow, miss, for the whole day. Please to give me a few minutes this evening." He advanced a step toward her; his voice faltered, and dropped timidly to a whisper. "I really have something to say to you, Miss Naomi. It would be a kindness on your part, a very, very great kindness, if you will let me say it before I rest to-night."

I rose again to resign my place to him. Once more Naomi checked me.

"No," she said. "Don't stir." She addressed John Jago very reluctantly: "If you are so much in earnest about it, Mr. John, I suppose it must be. I can't guess what you can possibly have to say to me which cannot be said before a third person. However, it wouldn't be civil, I suppose, to say 'No' in my place. You know it's my business to wind up the hall-clock at ten every night. If you choose to come and help me, the chances are that we shall have the hall to ourselves. Will that do?"

"Not in the hall, miss, if you will excuse me."

"Not in the hall!"

"And not in the house either, if I may make so bold."

"What do you mean?" She turned impatiently, and appealed to me. "Do you understand him?"

John Jago signed to me imploringly to let him answer for himself.

"Bear with me, Miss Naomi," he said. "I think I can make you understand me. There are eyes on the watch, and ears on the watch, in the house; and there are some footsteps, I won't say whose, so soft, that no person can hear them."

The last allusion evidently made itself understood. Naomi stopped him before he could say more.

"Well, where is it to be?" she asked, resignedly. "Will the garden do, Mr. John?"

"Thank you kindly, miss; the garden will do." He pointed to a gravel-walk beyond us, bathed in the full flood of the moonlight. "There," he said, "where we can see all round us, and be sure that nobody is listening. At ten o'clock." He paused, and addressed himself to me. "I beg to apologize, sir, for intruding myself on your conversation. Please to excuse me."

His eyes rested with a last anxious, pleading look on Naomi's face. He bowed to us, and melted away into the shadow of the tree. The distant sound of a door closed softly came to us through the stillness of the night. John Jago had re-entered the house.

Now that he was out of hearing, Naomi spoke to me very earnestly:

"Don't suppose, sir, I have any secrets with him," she said. "I know no more than you do what he wants with me. I have half a mind not to keep the appointment when ten o'clock comes. What would you do in my place?"

"Having made the appointment," I answered, "it seems to be due to yourself to keep it. If you feel the slightest alarm, I will wait in another part of the garden, so that I can hear if you call me."

She received my proposal with a saucy toss of the head, and a smile of pity for my ignorance.

"You are a stranger, Mr. Lefrank, or you would never talk to me in that way. In America, we don't do the men the honor of letting them alarm us. In America, the women take care of themselves. He has got my promise to meet him, as you say; and I must keep my promise. Only think," she added, speaking more to herself than to me, "of John Jago finding out Miss Meadowcroft's nasty, sly, underhand ways in the house! Most men would never have noticed her."

I was completely taken by surprise. Sad and severe Miss Meadowcroft a listener and a spy! What next at Morwick Farm?

"Was that hint at the watchful eyes and ears, and the soft footsteps, really an allusion to Mr. Meadowcroft's daughter?" I asked.

"Of course it was. Ah! she has imposed on you as she imposes on everybody else. The false wretch! She is secretly at the bottom of half the bad feeling among the men. I am certain of it - she keeps Mr. Meadowcroft's mind bitter toward the boys. Old as she is, Mr. Lefrank, and ugly as she is, she wouldn't object (if she could only make him ask her) to be John Jago's second wife. No, sir; and she wouldn't break her heart if the boys were not left a stick or a stone on the farm when the father dies. I have watched her, and I know it. Ah! I could tell you such things! But there's no time now, it's close on ten o'clock; we must say good-night. I am right glad I have spoken to you, sir. I say again, at parting, what I have said already: Use your influence, pray use your influence, to soften them, and to make them ashamed of themselves, in this wicked house. We will have more talk about what you can do to-morrow, when you are shown over the farm. Say good-by now. Hark! there is ten striking! And look! here is John Jago stealing out again in the shadow of the tree! Good-night, friend Lefrank; and pleasant dreams."

With one hand she took mine, and pressed it cordially; with the other she pushed me away without ceremony in the direction of the house. A charming girl - an irresistible girl! I was nearly as bad as the boys. I declare, I almost hated John Jago, too, as we crossed each other in the shadow of the tree.

Arrived at the glass door, I stopped and looked back at the gravelwalk.

They had met. I saw the two shadowy figures slowly pacing backward and forward in the moonlight, the woman a little in advance of the man. What was he saying to her? Why was he so anxious that not a word of it should be heard? Our presentiments are sometimes, in certain rare cases, the faithful prophecy of the future. A vague distrust of that moonlight meeting stealthily took a hold on my mind. "Will mischief come of it?" I asked myself as I closed the door and entered the house.

Mischief did come of it. You shall hear how.

CHAPTER IV. THE BEECHEN STICK.

Persons of sensitive, nervous temperament, sleeping for the first time in a strange house, and in a bed that is new to them, must make up their minds to pass a wakeful night. My first night at Morwick Farm was no exception to this rule. The little sleep I had was broken and disturbed by dreams. Toward six o'clock in the morning, my bed became unendurable to me. The sun was shining in brightly at the window. I determined to try the reviving influence of a stroll in the fresh morning air.

Just as I got out of bed, I heard footsteps and voices under my window.

The footsteps stopped, and the voices became recognizable. I had passed the night with my window open; I was able, without exciting notice from below, to look out.

The persons beneath me were Silas Meadowcroft, John Jago, and three strangers, whose dress and appearance indicated plainly enough that they were laborers on the farm. Silas was swinging a stout beechen stick in his hand, and was speaking to Jago, coarsely and insolently enough, of his moonlight meeting with Naomi on the previous night.

"Next time you go courting a young lady in secret," said Silas, "make sure that the moon goes down first, or wait for a cloudy sky. You were seen in the garden, Master Jago; and you may as well tell us the truth for once in a way. Did you find her open to persuasion, sir? Did she say 'Yes?'"

John Jago kept his temper.

"If you must have your joke, Mr. Silas," he said, quietly and firmly, "be pleased to joke on some other subject. You are quite wrong, sir, in what you suppose to have passed between the young lady and me."

Silas turned about, and addressed himself ironically to the three laborers.

"You hear him, boys? He can't tell the truth, try him as you may. He wasn't making love to Naomi in the garden last night oh dear, no! He has had one wife already; and he knows better than to take the yoke on his shoulders for the second time!"

Greatly to my surprise, John Jago met this clumsy jesting with a formal and serious reply.

"You are quite right, sir," he said. "I have no intention of marrying for the second time. What I was saying to Miss Naomi doesn't matter to you. It was not at all what you choose to suppose; it was something of quite another kind, with which you have no concern. Be pleased to understand once for all, Mr. Silas, that not so much as the thought of making love to the young lady has ever entered my head. I respect her; I admire her good qualities; but if she was the only woman left in the world, and if I was a much younger man than I am, I should never think of asking her to be my wife." He burst out suddenly into a harsh, uneasy laugh. "No, no! not my style, Mr. Silas, not my style!"

Something in those words, or in his manner of speaking them, appeared to exasperate Silas. He dropped his clumsy irony, and addressed himself directly to John Jago in a tone of savage contempt.

"Not your style?" he repeated. "Upon my soul, that's a cool way of putting it, for a man in your place! What do you mean by calling her 'not your style?' You impudent beggar! Naomi Colebrook is meat for your master!"

John Jago's temper began to give way at last. He approached defiantly a step or two nearer to Silas Meadowcroft.

"Who is my master?" he asked.

"Ambrose will show you, if you go to him," answered the other. "Naomi is _his_ sweetheart, not mine. Keep out of his way, if you want to keep a whole skin on your bones."

John Jago cast one of his sardonic side-looks at the farmer's wounded left hand. "Don't forget your own skin, Mr. Silas, when you threaten mine! I have set my mark on you once, sir. Let me by on my business, or I may mark you for a second time."

Silas lifted his beechen stick. The laborers, roused to some rude sense of the serious turn which the quarrel was taking, got between the two men, and parted them. I had been hurriedly dressing myself while the altercation was proceeding; and I now ran downstairs to try what my influence could do toward keeping the peace at Morwick Farm.

The war of angry words was still going on when I joined the men outside.

"Be off with you on your business, you cowardly hound!" I heard Silas say. "Be off with you to the town! and take care you don't meet Ambrose on the way!"

"Take you care you don't feel my knife again before I go!" cried the other man.

Silas made a desperate effort to break away from the laborers who were holding him.

"Last time you only felt my fist!" he shouted "Next time you shall feel this!"

He lifted the stick as he spoke. I stepped up and snatched it out of his hand.

"Mr. Silas," I said, "I am an invalid, and I am going out for a walk. Your stick will be useful to me. I beg leave to borrow it."

The laborers burst out laughing. Silas fixed his eyes on me with a stare of angry surprise. John Jago, immediately recovering his self-possession, took off his hat, and made me a deferential bow.

"I had no idea, Mr. Lefrank, that we were disturbing you," he said. "I am very much ashamed of myself, sir. I beg to apologize."

"I accept your apology, Mr. Jago," I answered, "on the understanding that you, as the older man, will set the example of forbearance if your temper is tried on any future occasion as it has been tried today. And I have further to request," I added, addressing myself to Silas, "that you will do me a favor, as your father's guest. The next time your good spirits lead you into making jokes at Mr. Jago's expense, don't carry them quite so far. I am sure you meant no harm, Mr. Silas. Will you gratify me by saying so yourself? I want to see you and Mr. Jago shake hands."

John Jago instantly held out his hand, with an assumption of good feeling which was a little overacted, to my thinking. Silas Meadowcroft made no advance of the same friendly sort on his side.

"Let him go about his business," said Silas. "I won't waste any more words on him, Mr. Lefrank, to please you. But (saving your presence) I'm damned if I take his hand!"

Further persuasion was plainly useless, addressed to such a man as this. Silas gave me no further opportunity of remonstrating with him, even if I had been inclined to do so. He turned about in sulky silence, and, retracing his steps along the path, disappeared round the corner of the house. The laborers withdrew next, in different directions, to begin the day's, work. John Jago and I were alone.

I left it to the man of the wild brown eyes to speak first.

"In half an hour's time, sir," he said, "I shall be going on business to Narrabee, our market-town here. Can I take any letters to the post for you? or is there anything else that I can do in the town?"

I thanked him, and declined both proposals. He made me another deferential bow, and withdrew into the house. I mechanically followed the path in the direction which Silas had taken before me.

Turning the corner of the house, and walking on for a little way, I found myself at the entrance to the stables, and face to face with Silas Meadowcroft once more. He had his elbows on the gate of the yard, swinging it slowly backward and forward, and turning and twisting a straw between his teeth. When he saw me approaching him, he advanced a step from the gate, and made an effort to excuse himself, with a very ill grace.

"No offense, mister. Ask me what you will besides, and I'll do it for you. But don't ask me to shake hands with John Jago; I hate him too badly for that. If I touched him with one hand, sir, I tell you this, I should throttle him with the other."

"That's your feeling toward the man, Mr. Silas, is it?"

"That's my feeling, Mr. Lefrank; and I'm not ashamed of it either."

"Is there any such place as a church in your neighborhood, Mr. Silas?"

"Of course there is."

"And do you ever go to it?"

"Of course I do."

"At long intervals, Mr. Silas?"

"Every Sunday, sir, without fail."

Some third person behind me burst out laughing; some third person had been listening to our talk. I turned round, and discovered Ambrose Meadowcroft.

"I understand the drift of your catechism, sir, though my brother doesn't," he said. "Don't be hard on Silas, sir. He isn't the only Christian who leaves his Christianity in the pew when he goes out of church. You will never make us friends with John Jago, try as you may. Why, what have you got there, Mr. Lefrank? May I die if it isn't my stick! I have been looking for it everywhere!"

The thick beechen stick had been feeling uncomfortably heavy in my invalid hand for some time past. There was no sort of need for my keeping it any longer. John Jago was going away to Narrabee, and Silas Meadowcroft's savage temper was subdued to a sulky repose. I handed the stick back to Ambrose. He laughed as he took it from me.

"You can't think how strange it feels, Mr. Lefrank, to be out without one's stick," he said. "A man gets used to his stick, sir; doesn't he? Are you ready for your breakfast?"

"Not just yet. I thought of taking a little walk first."

"All right, sir. I wish I could go with you; but I have got my work to do this morning, and Silas has his work too. If you go back by the way you came, you will find yourself in the garden. If you want to go further, the wicket-gate at the end will lead you into the lane."

Through sheer thoughtlessness, I did a very foolish thing. I turned back as I was told, and left the brothers together at the gate of the stable-yard.

CHAPTER V. THE NEWS FROM NARRABEE.

Arrived at the garden, a thought struck me. The cheerful speech and easy manner of Ambrose plainly indicated that he was ignorant thus far of the quarrel which had taken place under my window. Silas might confess to having taken his brother's stick, and might mention whose head he had threatened with it. It was not only useless, but undesirable, that Ambrose should know of the quarrel. I retraced my steps to the stable-yard. Nobody was at the gate. I called alternately to Silas and to Ambrose. Nobody answered. The brothers had gone away to their work.

Returning to the garden, I heard a pleasant voice wishing me "Good-morning." I looked round. Naomi Colebrook was standing at one of the lower windows of the farm. She had her working apron on, and she was industriously brightening the knives for the breakfast-table on an old-fashioned board. A sleek black cat balanced himself on her shoulder, watching the flashing motion of the knife as she passed it rapidly to and fro on the leather-covered surface of the board.

"Come here," she said; "I want to speak to you."

I noticed, as I approached, that her pretty face was clouded and anxious. She pushed the cat irritably off her shoulder; she welcomed me with only the faint reflection of her bright customary smile.

"I have seen John Jago," she said. "He has been hinting at something which he says happened under your bedroom window this morning. When I begged him to explain himself, he only answered, 'Ask Mr. Lefrank; I must be off to Narrabee.' What does it mean? Tell me right away, sir! I'm out of temper, and I can't wait!"

Except that I made the best instead of the worst of it, I told her what had happened under my window as plainly as I have told it here. She put down the knife that she was cleaning, and folded her hands before her, thinking.

"I wish I had never given John Jago that meeting," she said. "When a man asks anything of a woman, the woman, I find, mostly repents it if she says 'Yes.'"

She made that quaint reflection with a very troubled brow. The moonlight meeting had left some unwelcome remembrances in her mind. I saw that as plainly as I saw Naomi herself.

What had John Jago said to her? I put the question with all needful delicacy, making my apologies beforehand.

"I should like to tell you," she began, with a strong emphasis on the last word.

There she stopped. She turned pale; then suddenly flushed again to the deepest red. She took up the knife once more, and went on cleaning it as industriously as ever.

"I mustn't tell you," she resumed, with her head down over the knife. "I have promised not to tell anybody. That's the truth. Forget all about it, sir, as soon as you can. Hush! here's the spy who saw us last night on the walk and who told Silas!"

Dreary Miss Meadowcroft opened the kitchen door. She carried an ostentatiously large Prayer-book; and she looked at Naomi as only a jealous woman of middle age _can_ look at a younger and prettier woman than herself.

"Prayers, Miss Colebrook," she said in her sourest manner. She paused, and noticed me standing under the window. "Prayers, Mr. Lefrank," she added, with a look of devout pity, directed exclusively to my address.

"We will follow you directly, Miss Meadowcroft," said Naomi.

"I have no desire to intrude on your secrets Miss Colebrook."

With that acrid answer, our priestess took herself and her Prayer-book out of the kitchen. I joined Naomi, entering the room by the garden door. She met me eagerly. "I am not quite easy about something," she said. "Did you tell me that you left Ambrose and Silas together?"

"Yes."

"Suppose Silas tells Ambrose of what happened this morning?"

The same idea, as I have already mentioned, had occurred to my mind. I did my best to reassure Naomi.

"Mr. Jago is out of the way," I replied. "You and I can easily put things right in his absence."

She took my arm.

"Come in to prayers," she said. "Ambrose will be there, and I shall find an opportunity of speaking to him."

Neither Ambrose nor Silas was in the breakfast-room when we entered it. After waiting vainly for ten minutes, Mr. Meadowcroft told his daughter to read the prayers. Miss Meadowcroft read, thereupon, in the tone of an injured woman taking the throne of mercy by storm, and insisting on her rights. Breakfast followed; and still the brothers were absent. Miss Meadowcroft looked at her father, and said, "From bad to worse, sir. What did I tell you?" Naomi instantly applied the antidote: "The boys are no doubt detained over their work, uncle." She turned to me. "You want to see the farm, Mr. Lefrank. Come and help me to find the boys."

For more than an hour we visited one part of the farm after another, without discovering the missing men. We found them at last near the outskirts of a small wood, sitting, talking together, on the trunk of a felled tree.

Silas rose as we approached, and walked away, without a word of greeting or apology, into the wood. As he got on his feet, I noticed that his brother whispered something in his ear; and I heard him answer, "All right."

"Ambrose, does that mean you have something to keep a secret from us?" asked Naomi, approaching her lover with a smile. "Is Silas ordered to hold his tongue?"

Ambrose kicked sulkily at the loose stones lying about him. I noticed, with a certain surprise that his favorite stick was not in his hand, and was not lying near him.

"Business," he said in answer to Naomi, not very graciously "business between Silas and me. That's what it means, if you must know."

Naomi went on, woman-like, with her questioning, heedless of the reception which they might meet with from an irritated man.

"Why were you both away at prayers and breakfast-time?" she asked next.

"We had too much to do," Ambrose gruffly replied, "and we were too far from the house."

"Very odd," said Naomi. "This has never happened before since I have been at the farm."

"Well, live and learn. It has happened now."

The tone in which he spoke would have warned any man to let him alone. But warnings which speak by implication only are thrown away on women. The woman, having still something in her mind to say, said it.

"Have you seen anything of John Jago this morning?"

The smoldering ill-temper of Ambrose burst suddenly,why, it was impossible to guess--into a flame. "How many more questions am I to answer?" he broke out violently. "Are you the parson putting me through my catechism? I have seen nothing of John Jago, and I have got my work to go on with. Will that do for you?"

He turned with an oath, and followed his brother into the wood. Naomi's bright eyes looked up at me, flashing with indignation.

"What does he mean, Mr. Lefrank, by speaking to me in that way? Rude brute! How dare he do it?" She paused; her voice, look and manner suddenly changed. "This has never happened before, sir. Has anything gone wrong? I declare, I shouldn't know Ambrose again, he is so changed. Say, how does it strike you?"

I still made the best of a bad case.

"Something has upset his temper," I said. "The merest trifle, Miss Colebrook, upsets a man's temper sometimes. I speak as a man, and I know it. Give him time, and he will make his excuses, and all will be well again."

My presentation of the case entirely failed to re-assure my pretty companion. We went back to the house. Dinner-time came, and the brothers appeared. Their father spoke to them of their absence from morning prayers with needless severity, as I thought. They resented the reproof with needless indignation on their side, and left the room. A sour smile of satisfaction showed itself on Miss Meadowcroft's thin lips. She looked at her father; then raised her eyes sadly to the ceiling, and said, "We can only pray for them, sir."

Naomi disappeared after dinner. When I saw her again, she had some news for me.

"I have been with Ambrose," she said, "and he has begged my pardon. We have made it up, Mr. Lefrank. Still – still -"

"Still - what, Miss Naomi?"

"He is not like himself, sir. He denies it; but I can't help thinking he is hiding something from me."

The day wore on; the evening came. I returned to my French novel. But not even Dumas himself could keep my attention to the story. What else I was thinking of I cannot say. Why I was out of spirits I am unable to explain. I wished myself back in England: I took a blind, unreasoning hatred to Morwick Farm.

Nine o'clock struck; and we all assembled again at supper, with the exception of John Jago. He was expected back to supper; and we waited for him a quarter of an hour, by Mr. Meadowcroft's own directions. John Jago never appeared.

The night wore on, and still the absent man failed to return. Miss Meadowcroft volunteered to sit up for him. Naomi eyed her, a little maliciously I must own, as the two women parted for the night. I withdrew to my room; and again I was unable to sleep. When sunrise came, I went out, as before, to breathe the morning air.

On the staircase I met Miss Meadowcroft ascending to her own room. Not a curl of her stiff gray hair was disarranged; nothing about the impenetrable woman betrayed that she had been watching through the night.

"Has Mr. Jago not returned?" I asked.

Miss Meadowcroft slowly shook her head, and frowned at me.

"We are in the hands of Providence, Mr. Lefrank. Mr. Jago must have been detained for the night at Narrabee."

The daily routine of the meals resumed its unalterable course. Breakfast-time came, and dinner-time came, and no John Jago darkened the doors of Morwick Farm. Mr. Meadowcroft and his daughter consulted together, and determined to send in search of the missing man. One of the more intelligent of the laborers was dispatched to Narrabee to make inquiries.

The man returned late in the evening, bringing startling news to the farm. He had visited all the inns, and all the places of business resort in Narrabee; he had made endless inquiries in every direction, with this result--no one had set eyes on John Jago. Everybody declared that John Jago had not entered the town.

We all looked at each other, excepting the two brothers, who were seated together in a dark corner of the room. The conclusion appeared to be inevitable. John Jago was a lost man.

CHAPTER VI. THE LIMEKILN.

MR. MEADOWCROFT was the first to speak. "Somebody must find John," he said.

"Without losing a moment," added his daughter.

Ambrose suddenly stepped out of the dark corner of the room.

"I will inquire," he said.

Silas followed him.

"I will go with you," he added.

Mr. Meadowcroft interposed his authority.

"One of you will be enough; for the present, at least. Go you, Ambrose. Your brother may be wanted later. If any accident has happened (which God forbid!) we may have to inquire in more than one direction. Silas, you will stay at the farm."

The brothers withdrew together; Ambrose to prepare for his journey, Silas to saddle one of the horses for him. Naomi slipped out after them. Left in company with Mr. Meadowcroft and his daughter (both devoured by anxiety about the missing man, and both trying to conceal it under an assumption of devout resignation to circumstances), I need hardly add that I, too, retired, as soon as it was politely possible for me to leave the room. Ascending the stairs on my way to my own quarters, I discovered Naomi half hidden by the recess formed by an old-fashioned window-seat on the first landing. My bright little friend was in sore trouble. Her apron was over her face, and she was crying bitterly. Ambrose had not taken his leave as tenderly as usual. She was more firmly persuaded than ever that

"Ambrose was hiding something from her." We all waited anxiously for the next day. The next day made the mystery deeper than ever.

The horse which had taken Ambrose to Narrabee was ridden back to the farm by a groom from the hotel. He delivered a written message from Ambrose which startled us. Further inquiries had positively proved that the missing man had never been near Narrabee. The only attainable tidings of his whereabouts were tidings derived from vague report. It was said that a man like John Jago had been seen the previous day in a railway car, traveling on the line to New York. Acting on this imperfect information, Ambrose had decided on verifying the truth of the report by extending his inquiries to New York.

This extraordinary proceeding forced the suspicion on me that something had really gone wrong. I kept my doubts to myself; but I was prepared, from that moment, to see the disappearance of John Jago followed by very grave results.

The same day the results declared themselves.

Time enough had now elapsed for report to spread through the district the news of what had happened at the farm. Already aware of the bad feeling existing between the men, the neighbors had been now informed (no doubt by the laborers present) of the deplorable scene that had taken place under my bedroom window. Public opinion declares itself in America without the slightest reserve, or the slightest care for consequences. Public opinion declared on this occasion that the lost man was the victim of foul play, and held one or both of the brothers Meadowcroft responsible for his disappearance. Later in the day, the reasonableness of this serious view of the case was confirmed in the popular mind by a startling discovery. It was announced that a Methodist preacher lately settled at Morwick, and greatly respected throughout the district, had dreamed of John Jago in the character of a murdered man, whose bones were hidden at Morwick Farm. Before night the cry was general for a verification of the preacher's dream. Not only in the immediate district, but in the town of Narrabee itself, the public voice insisted on the necessity of a search for the mortal remains of John Jago at Morwick Farm.

In the terrible turn which matters had now taken, Mr. Meadowcroft the elder displayed a spirit and an energy for which I was not prepared.

"My sons have their faults," he said, "serious faults; and nobody knows it better than I do. My sons have behaved badly and ungratefully toward John Jago; I don't deny that, either. But Ambrose and Silas are not murderers. Make your search! I ask for it; no, I insist on it, after what has been said, in justice to my family and my name!"

The neighbors took him at his word. The Morwick section of the American nation organized itself on the spot. The sovereign people met in committee, made speeches, elected competent persons to represent the public interests, and began the search the next day. The whole proceeding, ridiculously informal from a legal point of view, was carried on by these extraordinary people with as stern and strict a sense of duty as if it had been sanctioned by the highest tribunal in the land.

Naomi met the calamity that had fallen on the household as resolutely as her uncle himself. The girl's courage rose with the call which was made on it. Her one anxiety was for Ambrose.

"He ought to be here," she said to me. "The wretches in this neighborhood are wicked enough to say that his absence is a confession of his guilt."

She was right. In the present temper of the popular mind, the absence of Ambrose was a suspicious circumstance in itself.

"We might telegraph to New York," I suggested, "if you only knew where a message would be likely to find him."

"I know the hotel which the Meadowcrofts use at New York," she replied. "I was sent there, after my father's death, to wait till Miss Meadowcroft could take me to Morwick."

We decided on telegraphing to the hotel. I was writing the message, and Naomi was looking over my shoulder, when we were startled by a strange voice speaking close behind us.

"Oh! that's his address, is it?" said the voice. "We wanted his address rather badly."

The speaker was a stranger to me. Naomi recognized him as one of the neighbors.

"What do you want his address for?" she asked, sharply.

"I guess we've found the mortal remains of John Jago, miss," the man replied. "We have got Silas already, and we want Ambrose too, on suspicion of murder."

"It's a lie!" cried Naomi, furiously "a wicked lie!"

The man turned to me.

"Take her into the next room, mister," he said, "and let her see for herself."

We went together into the next room.

In one corner, sitting by her father, and holding his hand, we saw stern and stony Miss Meadowcroft weeping silently. Opposite to them, crouched on the window-seat, his eyes wandering, his hands hanging helpless, we next discovered Silas Meadowcroft, plainly self-betrayed as a panic-stricken man. A few of the persons who had been engaged in the search were seated near, watching him. The mass of the strangers present stood congregated round a table in the middle of the room They drew aside as I approached with Naomi and allowed us to have a clear view of certain objects placed on the table.

The center object of the collection was a little heap of charred bones. Round this were ranged a knife, two metal buttons, and a stick partially burned. The knife was recognized by the laborers as the weapon John Jago habitually carried about with him - the weapon with which he had wounded Silas Meadowcroft's hand. The buttons Naomi herself declared to have a peculiar pattern on them, which had formerly attracted her attention to John Jago's coat. As for the stick, burned as it was, I had no difficulty in identifying the quaintly-carved knob at the top. It was the heavy beechen stick which I had snatched out of Silas's hand, and which I had restored to Ambrose on his claiming it as his own. In reply to my inquiries, I was informed that the bones, the knife, the buttons and the stick had all been found together in a limekiln then in use on the farm.

"Is it serious?" Naomi whispered to me as we drew back from the table.

It would have been sheer cruelty to deceive her now.

"Yes," I whispered back; "it is serious."

The search committee conducted its proceedings with the strictest regularity. The proper applications were made forthwith to a justice of the peace, and the justice issued his warrant. That night Silas was committed to prison; and an officer was dispatched to arrest Ambrose in New York.

For my part, I did the little I could to make myself useful. With the silent sanction of Mr. Meadowcroft and his daughter, I went to Narrabee, and secured the best legal assistance for the defense which the town could place at my disposal. This done, there was no choice but to wait for news of Ambrose, and for the examination before the magistrate which was to follow. I shall pass over the misery in the house during the interval of expectation; no useful purpose could be served by describing it now. Let me only say that Naomi's conduct strengthened me in the conviction that she possessed a noble nature. I was unconscious of the state of my own feelings at the time; but I am now disposed to think that this was the epoch at which I began to envy Ambrose the wife whom he had won.

The telegraph brought us our first news of Ambrose. He had been arrested at the hotel, and he was on his way to Morwick. The next day he arrived, and followed his brother to prison. The two were confined in separate cells, and were forbidden all communication with each other.

Two days later, the preliminary examination took place. Ambrose and Silas Meadowcroft were charged before the magistrate with the willful murder of John Jago. I was cited to appear as one of the witnesses; and, at Naomi's own request, I took the poor girl into court, and sat by her during the proceedings. My host also was present in his invalid-chair, with his daughter by his side.

Such was the result of my voyage across the ocean in search of rest and quiet; and thus did time and chance fulfill my first hasty foreboding of the dull life I was to lead at Morwick Farm!

CHAPTER VII. THE MATERIALS IN THE DEFENSE.

ON our way to the chairs allotted to us in the magistrate's court, we passed the platform on which the prisoners were standing together.

Silas took no notice of us. Ambrose made a friendly sign of recognition, and then rested his hand on the "bar" in front of him. As she passed beneath him, Naomi was just tall enough to reach his hand on tiptoe. She took it. "I know you are innocent," she whispered, and gave him one look of loving encouragement as she followed me to her place. Ambrose never lost his self-control. I may have been wrong; but I thought this a bad sign.

The case, as stated for the prosecution, told strongly against the suspected men.

Ambrose and Silas Meadowcroft were charged with the murder of John Jago (by means of the stick or by use of some other weapon), and with the deliberate destruction of the body by throwing it into the quicklime. In proof of this latter assertion, the knife which the deceased habitually carried about him, and the metal buttons which were known to belong to his coat, were produced. It was argued that these indestructible substances, and some fragments of the larger bones had alone escaped the action of the burning lime. Having produced medical witnesses to support this theory by declaring the bones to be human, and having thus circumstantially asserted the discovery of the remains in the kiln, the prosecution next proceeded to prove that the missing man had been murdered by the two brothers, and had been by them thrown into the quicklime as a means of concealing their guilt.

Witness after witness deposed to the inveterate enmity against the deceased displayed by Ambrose and Silas. The threatening language they habitually used toward him; their violent quarrels with him, which had become a public scandal throughout the neighborhood, and which had ended (on one occasion at least) in a blow; the disgraceful scene which had taken place under my window; and the restoration to Ambrose, on the morning of the fatal quarrel, of the very stick which had been found among the remains of the dead man--these facts and events, and a host of minor circumstances besides, sworn to by witnesses whose credit was unimpeachable, pointed with terrible directness to the conclusion at which the prosecution had arrived.

I looked at the brothers as the weight of the evidence pressed more and more heavily against them. To outward view at least, Ambrose still maintained his self-possession. It was far otherwise with Silas. Abject terror showed itself in his ghastly face; in his great knotty hands, clinging convulsively to the bar at which he stood; in his staring eyes, fixed in vacant horror on each witness who appeared. Public feeling judged him on the spot. There he stood, self-betrayed already, in the popular opinion, as a guilty man!

The one point gained in cross-examination by the defense related to the charred bones.

Pressed on this point, a majority of the medical witnesses admitted that their examination had been a hurried one; and that it was just possible that the bones might yet prove to be the remains of an animal, and not of a man. The presiding magistrate decided upon this that a second examination should be made, and that the member of the medical experts should be increased.

Here the preliminary proceedings ended. The prisoners were remanded for three days.

The prostration of Silas, at the close of the inquiry, was so complete, that it was found necessary to have two men to support him on his leaving the court. Ambrose leaned over the bar to speak to Naomi before he followed the jailer out. "Wait," he whispered, confidently, "till they hear what I have to say!" Naomi kissed her hand to him affectionately, and turned to me with the bright tears in her eyes.

"Why don't they hear what he has to say at once?" she asked. "Anybody can see that Ambrose is innocent. It's a crying shame, sir, to send him back to prison. Don't you think so yourself?"

If I had confessed what I really thought, I should have said that Ambrose had proved nothing to my mind, except that he possessed rare powers of self-control. It was impossible to acknowledge this to my little friend. I diverted her mind from the question of her lover's innocence by proposing that we should get the necessary order, and visit him in his prison on the next day. Naomi dried her tears, and gave me a little grateful squeeze of the hand.

"Oh my! what a good fellow you are!" cried the outspoken American girl. "When your time comes to be married, sir, I guess the woman won't repent saying yes to you!"

Mr. Meadowcroft preserved unbroken silence as we walked back to the farm on either side of his invalid-chair. His last reserves of resolution seemed to have given way under the overwhelming strain laid on them by the proceedings in court. His daughter, in stern indulgence to Naomi, mercifully permitted her opinion to glimmer on us only through the medium of quotation from Scripture texts. If the texts meant anything, they meant that she had foreseen all that had happened; and that the one sad aspect of the case, to her mind, was the death of John Jago, unprepared to meet his end.

I obtained the order of admission to the prison the next morning.

We found Ambrose still confident of the favorable result, for his brother and for himself, of the inquiry before the magistrate. He seemed to be almost as eager to tell, as Naomi was to hear, the true story of what had happened at the limekiln. The authorities of the prison, present, of course, at the interview, warned him to remember that what he said might be taken down in writing, and produced against him in court.

"Take it down, gentlemen, and welcome," Ambrose replied. "I have nothing to fear; I am only telling the truth."

With that he turned to Naomi, and began his narrative, as nearly as I can remember, in these words:

"I may as well make a clean breast of it at starting, my girl. After Mr. Lefrank left us that morning, I asked Silas how he came by my stick. In telling me how, Silas also told me of the words that had passed between him and John Jago under Mr. Lefrank's window. I was angry and jealous; and I own it freely, Naomi, I thought the worst that could be thought about you and John."

Here Naomi stopped him without ceremony.

"Was that what made you speak to me as you spoke when we found you at the wood?" she asked.

"Yes."

"And was that what made you leave me, when you went away to Narrabee, without giving me a kiss at parting?"

"It was."

"Beg my pardon for it before you say a word more."

"I beg your pardon."

"Say you are ashamed of yourself."

"I am ashamed of myself," Ambrose answered penitently.

"Now you may go on," said Naomi. "Now I'm satisfied."

Ambrose went on.

"We were on our way to the clearing at the other side of the wood while Silas was talking to me; and, as ill luck would have it, we took the path that led by the limekiln. Turning the corner, we met John Jago on his way to Narrabee. I was too angry, I tell you, to let him pass quietly. I gave him a bit of my mind. His blood was up too, I suppose; and he spoke out, on his side, as freely as I did. I own I threatened him with the stick; but I'll swear to it I meant him no harm. You know, after dressing Silas's hand, that John Jago is ready with his knife. He comes from out West, where they are always ready with one weapon or another handy in their pockets. It's likely enough he didn't mean to harm me, either; but how could I be sure of that? When he stepped up to me, and showed his weapon, I dropped the stick, and closed with him. With one hand I wrenched the knife away from him; and with the other I caught him by the collar of his rotten old coat, and gave him a shaking that made his bones rattle in his skin. A big piece of the cloth came away in my hand. I shied it into the quicklime close by us, and I pitched the knife after the cloth; and, if Silas hadn't stopped me, I think it's likely I might have shied John Jago himself into the lime next. As it was, Silas kept hold of me. Silas shouted out to him, 'Be off with you! and don't come back again, if you don't want to be burned in the kiln!' He stood looking at us for a minute, fetching his breath, and holding his torn coat round him. Then he spoke with a deadly-quiet voice and a deadly-quiet look: 'Many a true word, Mr. Silas,' he says, 'is spoken in jest. I shall not come back again.' He turned about, and left us. We stood staring at each other like a couple of fools. 'You don't think he means it?' I says. 'Bosh!' says Silas. 'He's too sweet on Naomi not to come back.' What's the matter now, Naomi?"

I had noticed it too. She started and turned pale, when Ambrose repeated to her what Silas had said to him.

"Nothing is the matter," Naomi answered. "Your brother has no right to take liberties with my name. Go on. Did Silas say any more while he was about it?"

"Yes; he looked into the kiln; and he says, 'What made you throw away the knife, Ambrose?' - 'How does a man know why he does anything,' I says, 'when he does it in a passion?' - 'It's a ripping good knife,' says Silas; 'in your place, I should have kept it.' I picked up the stick off the ground. 'Who says I've lost it yet?' I answered him; and with that I got up on the side of the kiln, and began sounding for the knife, to bring it, you know, by means of the stick, within easy reach of a shovel, or some such thing. 'Give us your hand,' I says to Silas. 'Let me stretch out a bit and I'll have it in no time.' Instead of finding the knife, I came nigh to falling myself into the burning lime. The vapor overpowered me, I suppose. All I know is, I turned giddy, and dropped the stick in the kiln. I should have followed the stick to a dead certainty, but for Silas pulling me back by the hand. 'Let it be,' says Silas. 'If I hadn't had hold of you, John Jago's knife would have been the death of you, after all!' He led me away by the arm, and we went on together on the road to the wood. We stopped where you found us, and sat down on the felled tree. We had a little more talk about John Jago. It ended in our agreeing to wait and see what happened, and to keep our own counsel in the meantime. You and Mr. Lefrank came upon us, Naomi, while we were still talking; and you guessed right when you guessed that we had a secret from you. You know the secret now."

There he stopped. I put a question to him - the first that I had asked yet.

"Had you or your brother any fear at that time of the charge which has since been brought against you?" I said.

"No such thought entered our heads, sir," Ambrose answered. "How could we foresee that the neighbors would search the kiln, and say what they have said of us? All we feared was, that the old man might hear of the quarrel, and be bitterer against us than ever. I was the more anxious of the two to keep things secret, because I had Naomi to consider as well as the old man. Put yourself in my place, and you will own, sir, that the prospect at home was not a pleasant one for me, if John Jago really kept away from the farm, and if it came out that it was all my doing."

(This was certainly an explanation of his conduct; but it was not satisfactory to my mind.)

"As you believe, then," I went on, "John Jago has carried out his threat of not returning to the farm? According to you, he is now alive, and in hiding somewhere?"

"Certainly!" said Ambrose.

"Certainly!" repeated Naomi.

"Do you believe the report that he was seen traveling on the railway to New York?"

"I believe it firmly, sir; and, what is more, I believe I was on his track. I was only too anxious to find him; and I say I could have found him if they would have let me stay in New York."

I looked at Naomi.

"I believe it too," she said. "John Jago is keeping away."

"Do you suppose he is afraid of Ambrose and Silas?"

She hesitated.

"He may be afraid of them," she replied, with a strong emphasis on the word "may."

"But you don't think it likely?"

She hesitated again. I pressed her again.

"Do you think there is any other motive for his absence?"

Her eyes dropped to the floor. She answered obstinately, almost doggedly,

"I can't say."

I addressed myself to Ambrose.

"Have you anything more to tell us?" I asked.

"No," he said. "I have told you all I know about it."

I rose to speak to the lawyer whose services I had retained. He had helped us to get the order of admission, and he had accompanied us to the prison. Seated apart he had kept silence throughout, attentively watching the effect of Ambrose Meadowcroft's narrative on the officers of the prison and on me.

"Is this the defense?" I inquired, in a whisper.

"This is the defense, Mr. Lefrank. What do you think, between ourselves?"

"Between ourselves, I think the magistrate will commit them for trial."

"On the charge of murder?"

"Yes, on the charge of murder."

CHAPTER VIII. THE CONFESSION.

My replies to the lawyer accurately expressed the conviction in my mind. The narrative related by Ambrose had all the appearance, in my eyes, of a fabricated story, got up, and clumsily got up, to pervert the plain meaning of the circumstantial evidence produced by the prosecution. I reached this conclusion reluctantly and regretfully, for Naomi's sake. I said all I could say to shake the absolute confidence which she felt in the discharge of the prisoners at the next examination.

The day of the adjourned inquiry arrived.

Naomi and I again attended the court together. Mr. Meadowcroft was unable, on this occasion, to leave the house. His daughter was present, walking to the court by herself, and occupying a seat by herself.

On his second appearance at the "bar," Silas was more composed, and more like his brother. No new witnesses were called by the prosecution. We began the battle over the medical evidence relating to the charred bones; and, to some extent, we won the victory. In other words, we forced the doctors to acknowledge that they differed widely in their opinions. Three confessed that they were not certain. Two went still further, and declared that the bones were the bones of an animal, not of a man. We made the most of this; and then we entered upon the defense, founded on Ambrose Meadowcroft's story.

Necessarily, no witnesses could be called on our side. Whether this circumstance discouraged him, or whether he privately shared my opinion of his client's statement, I cannot say. It is only certain that the lawyer spoke mechanically, doing his best, no doubt, but doing it without genuine conviction or earnestness on his own part. Naomi cast an anxious glance at me as he sat down. The girl's hand, as I took it, turned cold in mine. She saw plain signs of the failure of the defense in the look and manner of the counsel for the prosecution; but she waited resolutely until the presiding magistrate announced his decision. I had only too clearly foreseen what he would feel it to be his duty to do. Naomi's head dropped on my shoulder as he said the terrible words which committed Ambrose and Silas Meadowcroft to take their trial on the charge of murder.

I led her out of the court into the air. As I passed the "bar," I saw Ambrose, deadly pale, looking after us as we left him: the magistrate's decision had evidently daunted him. His brother Silas had dropped in abject terror on the jailer's chair; the miserable wretch shook and shuddered dumbly, like a cowed dog.

Miss Meadowcroft returned with us to the farm, preserving unbroken silence on the way back. I could detect nothing in her bearing which suggested any compassionate feeling for the prisoners in her stern and secret nature. On Naomi's withdrawal to her own room, we were left together for a few minutes; and then, to my astonishment, the outwardly merciless woman showed me that she, too, was one of Eve's daughters, and could feel and suffer, in her own hard way, like the rest of us. She suddenly stepped close up to me, and laid her hand on my arm.

"You are a lawyer, ain't you?" she asked.

"Yes."

"Have you had any experience in your profession?"

"Ten years' experience."

"Do _you_ think--" She stopped abruptly; her hard face softened; her eyes dropped to the ground. "Never mind," she said, confusedly. "I'm upset by all this misery, though I may not look like it. Don't notice me."

She turned away. I waited, in the firm persuasion that the unspoken question in her mind would sooner or later force its way to utterance by her lips. I was right. She came back to me unwillingly, like a woman acting under some influence which the utmost exertion of her will was powerless to resist.

"Do you believe John Jago is still a living man?"

She put the question vehemently, desperately, as if the words rushed out of her mouth in spite of her.

"I do not believe it," I answered.

"Remember what John Jago has suffered at the hands of my brothers," she persisted. "Is it not in your experience that he should take a sudden resolution to leave the farm?"

I replied, as plainly as before,

"It is not in my experience."

She stood looking at me for a moment with a face of blank despair; then bowed her gray head in silence, and left me. As she crossed the room to the door, I saw her look upward; and I heard her say to herself softly, between her teeth, "Vengeance is mine, I will repay, saith the Lord."

It was the requiem of John Jago, pronounced by the woman who loved him.

When I next saw her, her mask was on once more. Miss Meadowcroft was herself again. Miss Meadowcroft could sit by, impenetrably calm, while the lawyers discussed the terrible position of her brothers, with the scaffold in view as one of the possibilities of the "case."

Left by myself, I began to feel uneasy about Naomi. I went upstairs, and, knocking softly at her door, made my inquiries from outside. The clear young voice answered me sadly, "I am trying to bear it: I won't distress you when we meet again." I descended the stairs, feeling my first suspicion of the true nature of my interest in the American girl. Why had her answer brought the tears into my eyes? I went out, walking alone, to think undisturbedly. Why did the tones of her voice dwell on my ear all the way? Why did my hand still feel the last cold, faint pressure of her fingers when I led her out of court?

I took a sudden resolution to go back to England.

When I returned to the farm, it was evening. The lamp was not yet lighted in the hall. Pausing to accustom my eyes to the obscurity indoors, I heard the voice of the lawyer whom we had employed for the defense speaking to some one very earnestly.

"I'm not to blame," said the voice. "She snatched the paper out of my hand before I was aware of her."

"Do you want it back?" asked the voice of Miss Meadowcroft.

"No; it's only copy. If keeping it will help to quiet her, let her keep it by all means. Good evening."

Saying these last words, the lawyer approached me on his way out of the house. I stopped him without ceremony; I felt an ungovernable curiosity to know more.

"Who snatched the paper out of your hand?" I asked, bluntly.

The lawyer started. I had taken him by surprise. The instinct of professional reticence made him pause before he answered me.

In the brief interval of silence, Miss Meadowcroft replied to my question from the other end of the hall.

"Naomi Colebrook snatched the paper out of his hand."

"What paper?"

A door opened softly behind me. Naomi herself appeared on the threshold; Naomi herself answered my question.

"I will tell you," she whispered. "Come in here."

One candle only was burning in the room. I looked at her by the dim light. My resolution to return to England instantly became one of the lost ideas of my life.

"Good God!" I exclaimed, "what has happened now?"

She handed me the paper which she had taken from the lawyer's hand.

The "copy" to which he had referred was a copy of the written confession of Silas Meadowcroft on his return to prison. He accused his brother Ambrose of the murder of John Jago. He declared on his oath that he had seen his brother Ambrose commit the crime.

In the popular phrase, I could "hardly believe my own eyes." I read the last sentences of the confession for the second time:

"...I heard their voices at the limekiln. They were having words about Cousin Naomi. I ran to the place to part them. I was not in time. I saw Ambrose strike the deceased a terrible blow on the head with his (Ambrose's) heavy stick. The deceased dropped without a cry. I put my hand on his heart. He was dead. I was horribly frightened. Ambrose threatened to kill me next if I said a word to any living soul. He took up the body and cast it into the quicklime, and threw the stick in after it. We went on together to the wood. We sat down on a felled tree outside the wood. Ambrose made up the story that we were to tell if what he had done was found out. He made me repeat it after him, like a lesson. We were still at it when Cousin Naomi and Mr. Lefrank came up to us. They know the rest. This, on my oath, is a true confession. I make it of my own free-will, repenting me sincerely that I did not make it before."

(Signed)

"SILAS MEADOWCROFT."

I laid down the paper, and looked at Naomi once more. She spoke to me with a strange composure. Immovable determination was in her eye; immovable determination was in her voice.

"Silas has lied away his brother's life to save himself," she said. "I see cowardly falsehood and cowardly cruelty in every line on that paper. Ambrose is innocent, and the time has come to prove it."

"You forget," I said, "that we have just failed to prove it."

"John Jago is alive, in hiding from us and from all who know him," she went on. "Help me, friend Lefrank, to advertise for him in the newspapers."

I drew back from her in speechless distress. I own I believed that the new misery which had fallen on her had affected her brain.

"You don't believe it," she said. "Shut the door."

I obeyed her. She seated herself, and pointed to a chair near her.

"Sit down," she proceeded. "I am going to do a wrong thing; but there is no help for it. I am going to break a sacred promise. You remember that moonlight night when I met him on the garden walk?"

"John Jago?"

"Yes. Now listen. I am going to tell you what passed between John Jago and me."

CHAPTER IX. THE ADVERTISEMENT.

I WAITED in silence for the disclosure that was now to come. Naomi began by asking me a question.

"You remember when we went to see Ambrose in the prison?" she said.

"Perfectly."

"Ambrose told us of something which his villain of a brother said of John Jago and me. Do you remember what it was?"

I remembered perfectly. Silas had said, "John Jago is too sweet on Naomi not to come back."

"That's so," Naomi remarked when I had repeated the words. "I couldn't help starting when I heard what Silas had said; and I thought you noticed me."

"I did notice you."

"Did you wonder what it meant?"

"Yes."

"I'll tell you. It meant this: What Silas Meadowcroft said to his brother of John Jago was what I myself was thinking of John Jago at that very moment. It startled me to find my own thought in a man's mind spoken for me by a man. I am the person, sir, who has driven John Jago away from Morwick Farm; and I am the person who can and will bring him back again."

There was something in her manner, more than in her words, which let the light in suddenly on my mind.

"You have told me the secret," I said. "John Jago is in love with you."

"Mad about me!" she rejoined, dropping her voice to a whisper. "Stark, staring mad! that's the only word for him. After we had taken a few turns on the gravel-walk, he suddenly broke out like a man beside himself. He fell down on his knees; he kissed my gown, he kissed my feet; he sobbed and cried for love of me. I'm not badly off for courage, sir, considering I'm a woman. No man, that I can call to mind, ever really scared me before. But I own John Jago frightened me; oh my! he did frighten me! My heart was in my mouth, and my knees shook under me. I begged and prayed of him to get up and go away. No; there he knelt, and held by the skirt of my gown. The words poured out from him like--well, like nothing I can think of but water from a pump. His happiness and his life, and his hopes in earth and heaven, and Lord only knows what besides, all depended, he said, on a word from me. I plucked up spirit enough at that to remind him that I was promised to Ambrose. 'I think you ought to be ashamed of yourself,' I said, 'to own that you're wicked enough to love me when you know I am promised to another man!' When I spoke to him he took a new turn; he began abusing Ambrose. That straightened me up. I snatched my gown out of his hand, and I gave him my whole mind. 'I hate you!' I said. 'Even if I wasn't promised to Ambrose, I wouldn't marry you--no! not if there wasn't another man left in the world to ask me. I hate you, Mr. Jago! I hate you!' He saw I was in earnest at last. He got up from my feet, and he settled down quiet again, all on a sudden. 'You have said enough' (that was how he answered me). 'You have broken my life. I have no hopes and no prospects now. I had a pride in the farm, miss, and a pride in my work; I bore with your brutish cousins' hatred of me; I was faithful to Mr. Meadowcroft's interests; all for your sake, Naomi Colebrook, all for your sake! I have done with it now; I have done with my life at the farm. You will never be troubled with me again. I am going away, as the dumb creatures go when they are sick, to hide myself in a corner, and die. Do me one last favor. Don't make me the laughingstock of the whole neighborhood. I can't bear that; it maddens me only to think of it. Give me your promise never to tell any living soul what I have said to you to-night - your sacred promise to the man whose life you have broken!' I did as he bade me; I gave him my sacred promise with the tears in my eyes. Yes, that is so. After telling him I hated him (and I did hate him), I cried over his misery; I did! Mercy, what fools women are! What is the horrid perversity, sir, which makes us always ready to pity the men? He held out his hand to me; and he said, 'Good-by forever!' and I pitied him. I said, 'I'll shake hands with you if you will give me your promise in exchange for mine. I beg of you not to leave the farm. What will my uncle do if you go away? Stay here, and be friends with me, and forget and forgive, Mr. John.' He gave me his promise (he can refuse me nothing); and he gave it again when I saw him again the next morning. Yes. I'll do him justice, though I do hate him! I believe he honestly meant to keep his word as long as my eye was on him. It was only when he was left to himself that the Devil tempted him to break his promise and leave the farm. I was brought up to believe in the Devil, Mr. Lefrank; and I find it explains many things. It explains John Jago. Only let me find out where he has gone, and I'll engage he shall come back and clear Ambrose of the suspicion which his vile brother has cast on him. Here is the pen all ready for you. Advertise for him, friend Lefrank; and do it right away, for my sake!"

I let her run on, without attempting to dispute her conclusions, until she could say no more. When she put the pen into my hand, I began the composition of the advertisement as obediently as if I, too, believed that John Jago was a living man.

In the case of anyone else, I should have openly acknowledged that my own convictions remained unshaken. If no quarrel had taken place at the limekiln, I should have been quite ready, as I viewed the case, to believe that John Jago's disappearance was referable to the terrible disappointment which Naomi had inflicted on him. The same morbid dread of ridicule which had led him to assert that he cared nothing for Naomi, when he and Silas had quarreled under my bedroom window, might also have impelled him to withdraw himself secretly and suddenly from the scene of his discomfiture. But to ask me to believe, after what had happened at the limekiln, that he was still living, was to ask me to take Ambrose Meadowcroft's statement for granted as a true statement of facts.

I had refused to do this from the first; and I still persisted in taking that course. If I had been called upon to decide the balance of probability between the narrative related by Ambrose in his defense and the narrative related by Silas in his confession, I must have owned, no matter how unwillingly, that the confession was, to my mind, the least incredible story of the two.

Could I say this to Naomi? I would have written fifty advertisements inquiring for John Jago rather than say it; and you would have done the same, if you had been as fond of her as I was. I drew out the advertisement, for insertion in the Morwick Mercury, in these terms:

MURDER.--Printers of newspapers throughout the United States are desired to publish that Ambrose Meadowcroft and Silas Meadowcroft, of Morwick Farm, Morwick County, are committed for trial on the charge of murdering John Jago, now missing from the farm and from the neighborhood. Any person who can give information of the existence of said Jago may save the lives of two wrongly-accused men by making immediate communication. Jago is about five feet four inches high. He is spare and wiry; his complexion is extremely pale, his eyes are dark, and very bright and restless. The lower part of his face is concealed by a thick black beard and mustache. The whole appearance of the man is wild and flighty.

I added the date and the address. That evening a servant was sent on horseback to Narrabee to procure the insertion of the advertisement in the next issue of the newspaper.

When we parted that night, Naomi looked almost like her brighter and happier self. Now that the advertisement was on its way to the printing-office, she was more than sanguine: she was certain of the result.

"You don't know how you have comforted me," she said, in her frank, warm-hearted way, when we parted for the night. "All the newspapers will copy it, and we shall hear of John Jago before the week is out." She turned to go, and came back again to me. "I will never forgive Silas for writing that confession!" she whispered in my ear. "If he ever lives under the same roof with Ambrose again, I - well, I believe I wouldn't marry Ambrose if he did! There!"

She left me. Through the wakeful hours of the night my mind dwelt on her last words. That she should contemplate, under any circumstances, even the bare possibility of not marrying Ambrose, was, I am ashamed to say, a direct encouragement to certain hopes which I had already begun to form in secret. The next day's mail brought me a letter on business. My clerk wrote to inquire if there was any chance of my returning to England in time to appear in court at the opening of next law term. I answered, without hesitation, "It is still impossible for me to fix the date of my return." Naomi was in the room while I was writing. How would she have answered, I wonder, if I had told her the truth, and said, "You are responsible for this letter?"

CHAPTER X. THE SHERIFF AND THE GOVERNOR.

THE question of time was now a serious question at Morwick Farm. In six weeks the court for the trial of criminal cases was to be opened at Narrabee.

During this interval no new event of any importance occurred.

Many idle letters reached us relating to the advertisement for John Jago; but no positive information was received. Not the slightest trace of the lost man turned up; not the shadow of a doubt was cast on the assertion of the prosecution, that his body had been destroyed in the kiln. Silas Meadowcroft held firmly to the horrible confession that he had made. His brother Ambrose, with equal resolution, asserted his innocence, and reiterated the statement which he had already advanced. At regular periods I accompanied Naomi to visit him in the prison. As the day appointed for the opening of the court approached, he seemed to falter a little in his resolution; his manner became restless; and he grew irritably suspicious about the merest trifles. This change did not necessarily imply the consciousness of guilt: it might merely have indicated natural nervous agitation as the time for the trial drew near. Naomi noticed the alteration in her lover. It greatly increased her anxiety, though it never shook her confidence in Ambrose. Except at meal-times, I was left, during the period of which I am now writing, almost constantly alone with the charming American girl. Miss Meadowcroft searched the newspapers for tidings of the living John Jago in the privacy of her own room. Mr. Meadowcroft would see nobody but his daughter and his doctor, and occasionally one or two old friends. I have since had reason to believe that Naomi, in these days of our intimate association, discovered the true nature of the feeling with which she had inspired me. But she kept her secret. Her manner toward me steadily remained the manner of a sister; she never overstepped by a hair-breadth the safe limits of the character that she had assumed.

The sittings of the court began. After hearing the evidence, and examining the confession of Silas Meadowcroft, the grand jury found a true bill against both the prisoners. The day appointed for their trial was the first day in the new week.

I had carefully prepared Naomi's mind for the decision of the grand jury. She bore the new blow bravely.

"If you are not tired of it," she said, "come with me to the prison tomorrow. Ambrose will need a little comfort by that time." She paused, and looked at the day's letters lying on the table. "Still not a word about John Jago," she said. "And all the papers have copied the advertisement. I felt so sure we should hear of him long before this!"

"Do you still feel sure that he is living?" I ventured to ask.

"I am as certain of it as ever," she replied, firmly. "He is somewhere in hiding; perhaps he is in disguise. Suppose we know no more of him than we know now when the trial begins? Suppose the jury" She stopped, shuddering. Death, shameful death on the scaffold, might be the terrible result of the consultation of the jury. "We have waited for news to come to us long enough," Naomi resumed. "We must find the tracks of John Jago for ourselves. There is a week yet before the trial begins. Who will help me to make inquiries? Will you be the man, friend Lefrank!"

It is needless to add (though I knew nothing would come of it) that I consented to be the man.

We arranged to apply that day for the order of admission to the prison, and, having seen Ambrose, to devote ourselves immediately to the contemplated search. How that search was to be conducted was more than I could tell, and more than Naomi could tell. We were to begin by applying to the police to help us to find John Jago, and we were then to be guided by circumstances. Was there ever a more hopeless programme than this?

"Circumstances" declared themselves against us at starting. I applied, as usual, for the order of admission to the prison, and the order was for the first time refused; no reason being assigned by the persons in authority for taking this course. Inquire as I might, the only answer given was, "not today."

At Naomi's suggestion, we went to the prison to seek the explanation which was refused to us at the office. The jailer on duty at the outer gate was one of Naomi's many admirers. He solved the mystery cautiously in a whisper. The sheriff and the governor of the prison were then speaking privately with Ambrose Meadowcroft in his cell; they had expressly directed that no persons should be admitted to see the prisoner that day but themselves.

What did it mean? We returned, wondering, to the farm. There Naomi, speaking by chance to one of the female servants, made certain discoveries.

Early that morning the sheriff had been brought to Morwick by an old friend of the Meadowcrofts. A long interview had been held between Mr. Meadowcroft and his daughter and the official personage introduced by the friend. Leaving the farm, the sheriff had gone straight to the prison, and had proceeded with the governor to visit Ambrose in his cell. Was some potent influence being brought privately to bear on Ambrose? Appearances certainly suggested that inquiry. Supposing the influence to have been really exerted, the next question followed, What was the object in view? We could only wait and see.

Our patience was not severely tried. The event of the next day enlightened us in a very unexpected manner. Before noon, the neighbors brought startling news from the prison to the farm.

Ambrose Meadowcroft had confessed himself to be the murderer of John Jago! He had signed the confession in the presence of the sheriff and the governor on that very day.

I saw the document. It is needless to reproduce it here. In substance, Ambrose confessed what Silas had confessed; claiming, however, to have only struck Jago under intolerable provocation, so as to reduce the nature of his offense against the law from murder to manslaughter. Was the confession really the true statement of what had taken place? or had the sheriff and the governor, acting in the interests of the family name, persuaded Ambrose to try this desperate means of escaping the ignominy of death on the scaffold? The sheriff and the governor preserved impenetrable silence until the pressure put on them judicially at the trial obliged them to speak.

Who was to tell Naomi of this last and saddest of all the calamities which had fallen on her? Knowing how I loved her in secret, I felt an invincible reluctance to be the person who revealed Ambrose Meadowcroft's degradation to his betrothed wife. Had any other member of the family told her what had happened? The lawyer was able to answer me; Miss Meadowcroft had told her.

I was shocked when I heard it. Miss Meadowcroft was the last person in the house to spare the poor girl; Miss Meadowcroft would make the hard tidings doubly terrible to bear in the telling. I tried to find Naomi, without success. She had been always accessible at other times. Was she hiding herself from me now? The idea occurred to me as I was descending the stairs after vainly knocking at the door of her room. I was determined to see her. I waited a few minutes, and then ascended the stairs again suddenly. On the landing I met her, just leaving her room.

She tried to run back. I caught her by the arm, and detained her. With her free hand she held her handkerchief over her face so as to hide it from me.

"You once told me I had comforted you," I said to her, gently. "Won't you let me comfort you now?"

She still struggled to get away, and still kept her head turned from me.

"Don't you see that I am ashamed to look you in the face?" she said, in low, broken tones. "Let me go."

I still persisted in trying to soothe her. I drew her to the window-seat. I said I would wait until she was able to speak to me.

She dropped on the seat, and wrung her hands on her lap. Her downcast eyes still obstinately avoided meeting mine.

"Oh!" she said to herself, "what madness possessed me? Is it possible that I ever disgraced myself by loving Ambrose Meadowcroft?" She shuddered as the idea found its way to expression on her lips. The tears rolled slowly over her cheeks. "Don't despise me, Mr. Lefrank!" she said, faintly.

I tried, honestly tried, to put the confession before her in its least unfavorable light.

"His resolution has given way," I said. "He has done this, despairing of proving his innocence, in terror of the scaffold."

She rose, with an angry stamp of her foot. She turned her face on me with the deep-red flush of shame in it, and the big tears glistening in her eyes.

"No more of him!" she said, sternly. "If he is not a murderer, what else is he? A liar and a coward! In which of his characters does he disgrace me most? I have done with him forever!

I will never speak to him again!" She pushed me furiously away from her; advanced a few steps toward her own door; stopped, and came back to me. The generous nature of the girl spoke in her next words. "I am not ungrateful to you, friend Lefrank. A woman in my place is only a woman; and, when she is shamed as I am, she feels it very bitterly. Give me your hand! God bless you!"

She put my hand to her lips before I was aware of her, and kissed it, and ran back into her room.

I sat down on the place which she had occupied. She had looked at me for one moment when she kissed my hand. I forgot Ambrose and his confession; I forgot the coming trial; I forgot my professional duties and my English friends. There I sat, in a fool's elysium of my own making, with absolutely nothing in my mind but the picture of Naomi's face at the moment when she had last looked at me!

I have already mentioned that I was in love with her. I merely add this to satisfy you that I tell the truth.

CHAPTER XI. THE PEBBLE AND THE WINDOW.

MISS MEADOWCROFT and I were the only representatives of the family at the farm who attended the trial. We went separately to Narrabee. Excepting the ordinary greetings at morning and night, Miss Meadowcroft had not said one word to me since the time when I had told her that I did not believe John Jago to be a living man.

I have purposely abstained from encumbering my narrative with legal details. I now propose to state the nature of the defense in the briefest outline only.

We insisted on making both the prisoners plead not guilty. This done, we took an objection to the legality of the proceedings at starting. We appealed to the old English law, that there should be no conviction for murder until the body of the murdered person was found, or proof of its destruction obtained beyond a doubt. We denied that sufficient proof had been obtained in the case now before the court.

The judges consulted, and decided that the trial should go on.

We took our next objection when the confessions were produced in evidence. We declared that they had been extorted by terror, or by undue influence; and we pointed out certain minor particulars in which the two confessions failed to corroborate each other. For the rest, our defense on this occasion was, as to essentials, what our defense had been at the inquiry before the magistrate. Once more the judges consulted, and once more they overruled our objection. The confessions were admitted in evidence. On their side, the prosecution produced one new witness in support of their case. It is needless to waste time in recapitulating his evidence. He contradicted himself gravely on cross-examination. We showed plainly, and after investigation proved, that he was not to be believed on his oath.

The chief-justice summed up.

He charged, in relation to the confessions, that no weight should be attached to a confession incited by hope or fear; and he left it to the jury to determine whether the confessions in this case had been so influenced. In the course of the trial, it had been shown for the defense that the sheriff and the governor of the prison had told Ambrose, with his father's knowledge and sanction, that the case was clearly against him; that the only chance of sparing his family the disgrace of his death by public execution lay in making a confession; and that they would do their best, if he did confess, to have his sentence commuted to imprisonment for life. As for Silas, he was proved to have been beside himself with terror when he made his abominable charge against his brother. We had vainly trusted to the evidence on these two points to induce the court to reject the confessions: and we were destined to be once more disappointed in anticipating that the same evidence would influence the verdict of the jury on the side of mercy. After an absence of an hour, they returned into court with a verdict of "Guilty" against both the prisoners.

Being asked in due form if they had anything to say in mitigation of their sentence, Ambrose and Silas solemnly declared their innocence, and publicly acknowledged that their respective confessions had been wrung from them by the hope of escaping the hangman's hands. This statement was not noticed by the bench. The prisoners were both sentenced to death.

On my return to the farm, I did not see Naomi. Miss Meadowcroft informed her of the result of the trial. Half an hour later, one of the women-servants handed to me an envelope bearing my name on it in Naomi's handwriting.

The envelope inclosed a letter, and with it a slip of paper on which Naomi had hurriedly written these words: "For God's sake, read the letter I send to you, and do something about it immediately!"

I looked at the letter. It assumed to be written by a gentleman in New York. Only the day before, he had, by the merest accident, seen the advertisement for John Jago cut out of a newspaper and pasted into a book of "curiosities" kept by a friend. Upon this he wrote to Morwick Farm to say that he had seen a man exactly answering to the description of John Jago, but bearing another name, working as a clerk in a merchant's office in Jersey City. Having time to spare before the mail went out, he had returned to the office to take another look at the man before he posted his letter. To his surprise, he was informed that the clerk had not appeared at his desk that day. His employer had sent to his lodgings, and had been informed that he had suddenly packed up his hand-bag after reading the newspaper at breakfast; had paid his rent honestly, and had gone away, nobody knew where!

It was late in the evening when I read these lines. I had time for reflection before it would be necessary for me to act.

Assuming the letter to be genuine, and adopting Naomi's explanation of the motive which had led John Jago to absent himself secretly from the farm, I reached the conclusion that the search for him might be usefully limited to Narrabee and to the surrounding neighborhood.

The newspaper at his breakfast had no doubt given him his first information of the "finding" of the grand jury, and of the trial to follow. It was in my experience of human nature that he should venture back to Narrabee under these circumstances, and under the influence of his infatuation for Naomi. More than this, it was again in my experience, I am sorry to say, that he should attempt to make the critical position of Ambrose a means of extorting Naomi's consent to listen favorably to his suit. Cruel indifference to the injury and the suffering which his sudden absence might inflict on others was plainly implied in his secret withdrawal from the farm. The same cruel indifference, pushed to a further extreme, might well lead him to press his proposals privately on Naomi, and to fix her acceptance of them as the price to be paid for saving her cousin's life.

To these conclusions I arrived after much thinking. I had determined, on Naomi's account, to clear the matter up; but it is only candid to add that my doubts of John Jago's existence remained unshaken by the letter. I believed it to be nothing more nor less than a heartless and stupid "hoax."

The striking of the hall-clock roused me from my meditations. I counted the strokes - midnight!

I rose to go up to my room. Everybody else in the farm had retired to bed, as usual, more than an hour since. The stillness in the house was breathless. I walked softly, by instinct, as I crossed the room to look out at the night. A lovely moonlight met my view; it was like the moonlight on the fatal evening when Naomi had met John Jago on the garden walk.

My bedroom candle was on the side-table; I had just lighted it. I was just leaving the room, when the door suddenly opened, and Naomi herself stood before me!

Recovering the first shook of her sudden appearance, I saw instantly in her eager eyes, in her deadly-pale cheeks, that something serious had happened. A large cloak was thrown over her; a white handkerchief was tied over her head. Her hair was in disorder; she had evidently just risen in fear and in haste from her bed.

"What is it?" I asked, advancing to meet her.

She clung, trembling with agitation, to my arm.

"John Jago!" she whispered.

You will think my obstinacy invincible. I could hardly believe it, even then!

"Where?" I asked.

"In the back-yard," she replied, "under my bedroom window!"

The emergency was far too serious to allow of any consideration for the small proprieties of every-day life.

"Let me see him!" I said.

"I am here to fetch you," she answered, in her frank and fearless way. "Come upstairs with me."

Her room was on the first floor of the house, and was the only bedroom which looked out on the back-yard. On our way up the stairs she told me what had happened.

"I was in bed," she said, "but not asleep, when I heard a pebble strike against the window-pane. I waited, wondering what it meant. Another pebble was thrown against the glass. So far, I was surprised, but not frightened. I got up, and ran to the window to look out. There was John Jago looking up at me in the moonlight!"

"Did he see you?"

"Yes. He said, 'Come down and speak to me! I have something serious to say to you!'"

"Did you answer him?"

"As soon as I could catch my breath, I said, 'Wait a little,' and ran downstairs to you. What shall I do?"

"Let me see him, and I will tell you."

We entered her room. Keeping cautiously behind the window-curtain, I looked out.

There he was! His beard and mustache were shaved off; his hair was close cut. But there was no disguising his wild, brown eyes, or the peculiar movement of his spare, wiry figure, as he walked slowly to and fro in the moonlight waiting for Naomi. For the moment, my own agitation almost overpowered me; I had so firmly disbelieved that John Jago was a living man!

"What shall I do?" Naomi repeated.

"Is the door of the dairy open?" I asked.

"No; but the door of the tool-house, round the corner, is not locked."

"Very good. Show yourself at the window, and say to him, 'I am coming directly.'"

The brave girl obeyed me without a moment's hesitation.

There had been no doubt about his eyes and his gait; there was no doubt now about his voice, as he answered softly from below "All right!"

"Keep him talking to you where he is now," I said to Naomi, "until I have time to get round by the other way to the tool-house. Then pretend to be fearful of discovery at the dairy, and bring him round the corner, so that I can hear him behind the door."

We left the house together, and separated silently. Naomi followed my instructions with a woman's quick intelligence where stratagems are concerned. I had hardly been a minute in the tool-house before I heard him speaking to Naomi on the other side of the door.

The first words which I caught distinctly related to his motive for secretly leaving the farm. Mortified pride, doubly mortified by Naomi's contemptuous refusal and by the personal indignity offered to him by Ambrose, was at the bottom of his conduct in absenting himself from Morwick. He owned that he had seen the advertisement, and that it had actually encouraged him to keep in hiding!

"After being laughed at and insulted and denied, I was glad," said the miserable wretch, "to see that some of you had serious reason to wish me back again. It rests with you, Miss Naomi, to keep me here, and to persuade me to save Ambrose by showing myself and owning to my name."

"What do you mean?" I heard Naomi ask, sternly.

He lowered his voice; but I could still hear him.

"Promise you will marry me," he said, "and I will go before the magistrate to-morrow, and show him that I am a living man."

"Suppose I refuse?"

"In that case you will lose me again, and none of you will find me till Ambrose is hanged."

"Are you villain enough, John Jago, to mean what you say?" asked the girl, raising her voice.

"If you attempt to give the alarm," he answered, "as true as God's above us, you will feel my hand on your throat! It's my turn now, miss; and I am not to be trifled with. Will you have me for your husband - yes or no?"

"No!" she answered, loudly and firmly.

I burst open the door, and seized him as he lifted his hand on her. He had not suffered from the nervous derangement which had weakened me, and he was the stronger man of the two. Naomi saved my life. She struck up his pistol as he pulled it out of his pocket with his free hand and presented it at my head. The bullet was fired into the air. I tripped up his heels at the same moment The report of the pistol had alarmed the house. We two together kept him on the ground until help arrived.

CHAPTER XII. THE END OF IT.

JOHN JAGO was brought before the magistrate, and John Jago was identified the next day.

The lives of Ambrose and Silas were, of course, no longer in peril, so far as human justice was concerned. But there were legal delays to be encountered, and legal formalities to be observed, before the brothers could be released from prison in the characters of innocent men.

During the interval which thus elapsed, certain events happened which may be briefly mentioned here before I close my narrative.

Mr. Meadowcroft the elder, broken by the suffering which he had gone through, died suddenly of a rheumatic affection of the heart. A codicil attached to his will abundantly justified what Naomi had told me of Miss Meadowcroft's influence over her father, and of the end she had in view in exercising it. A life income only was left to Mr. Meadowcroft's sons. The freehold of the farm was bequeathed to his daughter, with the testator's recommendation added, that she should marry his "best and dearest friend, Mr. John Jago."

Armed with the power of the will, the heiress of Morwick sent an insolent message to Naomi, requesting her no longer to consider herself one of the inmates at the farm. Miss Meadowcroft, it should be here added, positively refused to believe that John Jago had ever asked Naomi to be his wife, or had ever threatened her, as I had heard him threaten her, if she refused. She accused me, as she accused Naomi, of trying meanly to injure John Jago in her estimation, out of hatred toward "that much-injured man;" and she sent to me, as she had sent to Naomi, a formal notice to leave the house.

We two banished ones met the same day in the hall, with our traveling-bags in our hands.

"We are turned out together, friend Lefrank," said Naomi, with her quaintly-comical smile. "You will go back to England, I guess; and I must make my own living in my own country. Women can get employment in the States if they have a friend to speak for them. Where shall I find somebody who can give me a place?"

I saw my way to saying the right word at the right moment.

"I have got a place to offer you," I replied.

She suspected nothing, so far.

"That's lucky, sir," was all she said. "Is it in a telegraph-office or in a dry-goods store?"

I astonished my little American friend by taking her then and there in my arms, and giving her my first kiss.

"The office is by my fireside," I said; "the salary is anything in reason you like to ask me for; and the place, Naomi, if you have no objection to it, is the place of my wife."

I have no more to say, except that years have passed since I spoke those words and that I am as fond of Naomi as ever.

Some months after our marriage, Mrs. Lefrank wrote to a friend at Narrabee for news of what was going on at the farm. The answer informed us that Ambrose and Silas had emigrated to New Zealand, and that Miss Meadowcroft was alone at Morwick Farm. John Jago had refused to marry her. John Jago had disappeared again, nobody knew where.